THE WO...
THE WOLVES

M. NOVAK

The Casting

It was in one of those previously derelict buildings that had been revamped and converted into offices and studios, lots of studios. Arty types gravitated to the area at that time; photographers, designers of all kinds. Advertising agencies flocked there and set up residence. Hard, brutal surfaces abounded everywhere, concrete and metal.

One of the bigger advertising agencies had organised the casting.

The queue of girls laced down three floors of clanging iron stairs, painted black. Ceci was reminded of climbing similar, perilously slippery stairs, as a child, to get to the top of a plastic tube which she would slide down and splash into a pool. Inside the plastic tube there would be ridges to graze the skin.

"I thought this was for a modelling job." commented the girl on the step beneath Ceci. They were approaching the junction of the second floor. Ceci, deep in her thoughts, stared at the girl.

"It is, it's for a new brand."

"Doing what for a new brand? Have you seen this lot?" The girl's voice was dismissive, scornful.

Ceci felt itchy with discomfort. The waistband of her tight jeans was digging into the flesh of her bloated stomach.

"What do you mean? What's wrong with them?" Ceci peered at the girls that were visible to her, looking down through the metal railings. They looked just like her, she thought, tallish, thinnish, prettier than average, their books clutched under their arms. Some of them sat or crouched, bored on the uncomfortable stairs, chewing gum or smoking.

The other girl snorted dismissively and Ceci narrowed her eyes at her.

Mean. She thought.

"They're not tall enough, and a lot of them are too tarty. This will be for some dodgy shit, you wait."

The mean girl was very tall and skinny. Hot pants and a black vest top. Collar bones sharp as knives. Huge dark eyes and wide, flaky dry lips.

Editorial, thought Ceci, and she was right, the others, now that she was observing them closely through a critical lens were…

"Tacky, promo girls." The girl lit a cigarette. They happened to be passing an open window. Summer in London and the humidity entered, sticky as a second skin.

"I'm a tacky promo girl too." Muttered Ceci.

"What?"

"I said…"

"I heard you, but no, you're not tacky, no bleached hair or extensions, nor lip implants…you're just…ordinary…"

"Thanks." Ceci smirked bitterly.

"I'm Nicole." Said the girl and then carried on speaking, not waiting to hear Ceci's name. "These things…you realise there's no point in waiting after thirty minutes, because it's for some crap that you'll never get and sometimes, like now, don't even want, but then you think, hell, you're here now, do you know what I mean? There's no point in moving. It's cold, you're hungry, maybe you can't face trying to find the next place. Sometimes you stay in the queue just to have a rest."

Good grief. Ceci stared at the girl. It's not cold, not even slightly, she thought.

"Did you come far?" She asked finally, politely.

"What are you, my mother?" Nicole scoffed. "Actually, my mother would never sound that posh. You have a teacher thing going on, is your mum a teacher?"

"What? No! I…"

"I'm only kidding! Not that far actually, I live in Vauxhall. It's pretty easy for me to get to all these places. I'm in a bad mood, ignore me."

It was too late for that. They talked a bit about their respective agencies. As Ceci suspected, Nicole was with a far better, well-known, modelling agency and had done lots of editorial stuff.

"What on earth are you doing here?" She asked her, baffled.

"You know editorial pays shit, right? I mean yeah, you get some great pics, but the money is rubbish. This job, on the other hand, is weirdly well paid. I need the money, I'm not going to lie."

"I don't really know what it's for." Admitted Ceci, "A big brand, yes, lots of money, but they never said which one nor what the job was."

"Yes." Nicole exhaled smoke over Ceci's head. "Suspicious!" She smirked. They had passed the window by then and were approaching the third floor.

"I think the end is in sight." Ceci smiled relieved. Just above them, she saw a girl walk through a door, someone unseen asked her name, her agency.

"You shouldn't wear jeans you know." Nicole observed in a contemplative fashion.

"Why not?" Ceci felt a fine mist of depression settle over her.

"Do they make me look fat?"

"No! It's summer, they make you look too hot! Not in a sexy way, but in an overheated way."

"I guess you're right, but shorts…" Ceci stared at Nicole's legs with unconcealed envy. "Put it this way, I don't look like you do in shorts, trust me."

"Pfft!" Nicole waved the hand with the cigarette dismissively.

"Skinny isn't everything…you wait, it won't be sufficient for whatever this is…"

"Sufficient?" Ceci raised her eyebrows at Nicole, perplexed, "What do you mean?"

"I mean this won't be the sort of job where being tall and skinny and being a great clothes horse count for anything, that's all."

"Oh, OK." Ceci chuckled, "You make it sound kind of sinister!"

"It can't be, can it, be a fashion modelling type of job?" Nicole said in a low, contemplative voice as she chucked her cigarette butt out of the third-floor window.

"If they wanted anything dodgy, they would call escort agencies not model agencies, wouldn't they?" Ceci retorted, almost defensively. Nicole smirked, quietly muttered something about a fine line.

They had arrived, by then, in front of the metal door on the third-floor landing. A young woman with a clipboard was ticking off their names and agencies.

"Ceci," announced Ceci, "with a 'c,' from Spark."

Behind her Ceci thought she could imagine Nicole sneer at the name of the subpar agency, and involuntarily, she felt herself redden. She thought she could smell the tang of old sweat, and she further imagined that it came from her, Ceci, overdressed and overheated in jeans on a roasting day in central London.

The room was spacious, rectangular, and devoid of furniture except for a trestle table and three people sitting behind it at the far end. Ceci walked towards it, heavily, self-consciously, clutching her portfolio with one sweaty hand.

Two men and a woman, all polished. They looked fashionable, superficially pleasant. The woman a bit older, a scar snaking down her neck loosely covered with a pale chiffon scarf. One of the men had an orange tan, fake looking, maybe applied from a bottle. Around his eyes, there were white rings as if from sunglasses.

Ceci, exhausted suddenly, glanced at them all and then lowered her gaze towards the wooden floor; bare boards painted white.

It was the third man that spoke, the plainest, but the jolliest. His voice had the cadence, the tone of a town jester. He sounded like a primary school teacher chivvying his charges along.

Ceci's mum was a nursery school teacher and Ceci was familiar with the tone. It was funny how Nicole had guessed.

"This job calls for an outgoing, smiley sort of personality. Someone who can go with the flow! Do you think you possess those qualities?" He grinned at Ceci who was standing in front of the table then. Her book was open in front of them but they were barely looking at it.

"Yes, I…yes…but what is the job exactly?"

"We can't provide you yet with the name of the client, there's a new strategy in place."

"A strategy?"

"Yes, we are going to create, around the product an air of mystery by sending teams of girls out around the country and going into pubs."

"To give out the product?" Ceci was mystified.

The grinning man sighed. He must, thought Ceci, be sick to death of explaining this to every single model at the casting.

"No, not the product itself, the girls will be giving out plain t-shirts with a question marks on them. The aim is to get people talking even before the product is officially launched."

"Ah,OK. I see, I think."

"So, friendliness, ability to travel, willingness to adapt are the most significant qualities we are looking for…being photogenic not so relevant for this one, which is why we're not really looking at your books…so…" The grin again. It was sparkling white, he had a rich person's teeth.

"Are you smiley and friendly, that is the question?"

Nicole

"Did you get it then?" Her mum's voice thundered through from the living room as soon as Nicole had let herself into the flat. Going just by the powerful timbre of that voice, one would never have imagined that Chantal was an invalid.

Nicole had been thinking that she didn't even mind the estate in the summer when it was sunny. Walking through the communal areas, with the small children shrieking happily and playing on the grass, it seemed almost like a different, better place. There was a friendly, holiday type of vibe.

 A few weeks ago, volunteers from some charity, cheerful, chatty ladies with litter pickers had wandered about cleaning and removing evidence of drug use. There had been dark murmurings from the longtime residents about how it was just for show, that it was pointless and merely symbolic, but Nicole, personally was glad of them. Even if the results were just temporary, which of course they were; it was better than nothing.

The current lengthy hours of daylight made everything better, everyone safer, that was obvious.

The danger was in the gangs and the gang members were like vampires, they only emerged as the darkness descended. Nicole imagined them itching to escape the stifling, foul smelling confines of their own flats, also on the estate, almost all of them. Addicts most, except one or two of the psychos at the top of the food chain, who got their kicks from the control and the money. The others were their dependants, for everything.

As tiny kids, they would all idolize the gangs which seemed to symbolise freedom, money, glamour, power; all the things woefully lacking in their own small lives. Only once deeply entrenched, did the unwitting recruits realise that firstly, the perks were mainly just for the top dogs, and secondly, they would be too busy chasing their next fix to appreciate any of it.

Nicole had gone to school with nearly all of the young people on the estate, gang members and otherwise. They knew her by sight, but nowadays, and after what had happened, the ones that remained from that era, tended to ignore her which suited Nicole just fine.

Still, Nicole barricaded herself and her mother, Chantal, into the flat at night. She wasn't taking any chances.

That evening, as usual, she turned to face the heavy door, as soon as she entered the flat. She drew the bolts across, counting them as she went, there were five of them. They were thick and heavy and just dragging them across caused her muscles to ache. Chantal hadn't been strong enough to do it in years. Afterwards, Nicole went into the living room and there was her mother on her usual recliner, the air stuffy and pungent, sour with the trapped odours of food and summer sweat, dust motes everywhere.

Nicole sighed heavily and headed over to open a window. Instantly, the high voices of the children wafted in.

"Well?" asked Chantal, "Answer me, young lady when I talk to you!"

"I've told you countless times, mum, rarely do we hear straight away, mostly the agency tells us the next day if we got it, so, I don't know yet. Anyway, that casting was busy, half of London was there!"

"For a show, was it? Which one?"

Nicole's mother was under the impression that all modelling involved the catwalk, and to be fair, most of Nicole's modelling had, to date, involved the catwalk. Even with her editorial work, as Chantal would have found most of Nicole's pictures baffling if not outright alarming, it was usually better just to pretend all her jobs were, in fact, catwalk shows.

"This one would mean travelling, if I got it." Nicole told her mother then.

"Travelling?"

"Yes, I know, not ideal, if it happens, maybe we could ask Brenda to sleep over?"

Brenda was Chantal's friend from church, a pious, tedious kind of lady but kindly. She would always step in to help Nicole's mum if Nicole wasn't around. She considered it her duty. It was also her duty to make sure to accompany Chantal to church every week without fail.

"Hmmm, is this job worth that? I mean is it good money?"

"It is as it happens, otherwise I would not consider leaving you. Anyway, chances are I won't get it. I think they were looking at blondes…"

Blonde tarts, Nicole thought, but of course did not say.

Chantal had been incapacitated by a stroke a few years ago and now found it very difficult to move independently. Except for weekly visits to church with Brenda and rare visits from other old friends, she spent her time slumped in her tatty recliner watching TV in the living room, and depended on Nicole for virtually everything.

Nicole, somewhere in the murky depths of her conscience, regarded it as her penance. Her mother might well have had the stroke because of what had happened, because of what she, Nicole had done. It might have been her fault.

The doctors had always said that it didn't work like that, but Nicole wasn't sure. In any case, her mum was her responsibility now; she had to look after her and the pair of them always needed money. That was one thing there was never enough of.

"You're getting older now," mumbled her mum then with her face lowered towards her chest, as if talking to herself, "Sooner or later, you'll have to leave, you can't be babysitting me forever."

Ceci

"Cecilia!" Ceci's boyfriend tended to call her that when he was annoyed with her, which lately had been more often than not.

The couple lived together in a studio flat in Kentish town. It had seemed like a bargain when they had found it six months ago, but now Ceci was of the opinion that living there was like residing in a cage or a prison. Or possibly, that was because she was beginning to realise that Stuart, her boyfriend, was not, actually, much fun to live with, not at all.

 That was an understatement, in fact. He was bossy and controlling and wanted to know the precise details of every single casting and job that she did. Not in a casual interested way either, but in a suspicious way.

Stuart worked as a freelance electrician, he managed his own schedule, so he had plenty of time on his hands.

"It's just because I worry about you and want to protect you!" He would always exclaim, in an annoying petulant voice, after grilling her about exactly where she had been and who she had spoken to.

Before they had moved in together, Stuart's protective nature had seemed charming and loving. Ceci was from a large, chaotic family in Leeds and she had suffered, during her childhood, from a type of friendly, benign neglect. When she met Stuart (he had come to fix the electrics in a rundown flat that Ceci had shared with a couple of girls when she first moved to London), being the focus of so much attention had flooded Ceci with endorphins. Being cared for and protected had seemed appealing.

Stuart's love was exactly like a drug.

It took her a while to see the flip side and now, a year later, she was seeing it every day.

That day he called out to her before she had even entered the room. Because, of course, it was just a room they lived in. A double bed at one end, a makeshift 'kitchen' at the other, just a burner stove, a camping fridge, and a sink. The bathroom was alright to be fair. Compact, but the shower unit was the best part of the whole living arrangement. Ceci would have spent all her time in there with the door locked if it wasn't for the water bills.

"Cecilia, your agency called." Stuart was standing barefoot on the worn carpet in the area between the bed and the kitchen. He had his hands on his hips. Ceci could see that his biceps were tensed.

"They said to tell you that you got the job. I asked what job that was and they said the *travelling* job." He stopped there to glare at Ceci, making sure she realised the full extent of her transgression.

"You didn't think to tell me that you were going for a job that involved *travelling*?"

Ceci sighed deeply. She felt very close to tears. The journey home from the casting had been stifling and uncomfortable. Rush hour in London and the tube was packed and not air-conditioned. More than once, Ceci had felt as if she would pass out. In addition to that, her stomach was cramping against the confines of her tight jeans. There was nothing she wanted to do more than pull them off and stand for hours in the shower, or even sit in there, because she still felt a bit weak and dizzy, but she couldn't do that with Stuart right there in her face and itching for a fight.

"I didn't tell you," Ceci started to explain, her voice wavering with misery, "Because I only ever get jobs from a tiny percentage of castings that I attend, and I never would have thought I'd get this one, there were SO many girls there!"

She should have been allowed to be glad she got the job. He should have been glad. That would have been the normal reaction. A sadness came to her then, all-encompassing and dark. This was shit. This situation was untenable. This relationship was awful. She had a sudden desperate urge to tell him to leave, then and there but she couldn't because they each paid half of the rent and neither could afford it individually, and she was pretty certain that he had nowhere to go. He didn't seem to have many friends in London, any really.

That should have rung some alarm bells for a start. What sort of person didn't have any friends?

Also, and crucially, Ceci was a bit afraid of Stuart. He had never yet hit her, to be fair, but the potential seemed to be there always, bubbling away just beneath his skin. The potential for violence. There was this look he got, this cold empty look, when he was furious. He had it then.

"Look my stomach is killing me, I'm just going to get in the shower, OK?"

He had been edging towards her slowly, looming over her. He wasn't much taller but there was a bulkiness to him and he seemed to take up far more room.

He stopped then though. He seemed taken aback. He could hardly take issue with her stomach cramping although no doubt in time he might try.

Training Day

Nicole saw Ceci straight away in the hotel lobby. One day training for the mysterious job was to be held in a conference room in an anonymous hotel chain. The lobby was teeming with girls. The majority were, in fact, blonde. And trashy looking, Nicole thought to herself with an unkind smirk.

Nevertheless, she was very pleased to see a familiar face.

"So glad you made it through!" She grinned at Ceci, who looked strangely glum, her skin pale and drawn beneath her make-up.

"I can't wait for the travelling to commence, do you know when it's supposed to start?" She asked in a small, tight voice.

"I know exactly what I knew after the casting, basically nothing! I am so surprised to have got through…I mean, just look at this lot!"

Ceci turned to look at the crowd Nicole was indicating and chuckled. As had been obvious at the casting, this was not a high-fashion cohort, Nicole was by far the tallest and thinnest. Most had bleached hair and their faces were shades of orange from liberally applied fake tan. They wore hot pants and crop tops and bright lipstick and fake eyelashes.

"I mean, the things we do for money, eh?" Remarked Nicole drily, sucking on a cigarette.

"As long as it's not too much!" Ceci rolled her eyes.

Nicole studied her with her own eyes narrowed. "You seem different today, more, I don't know, cynical?"

"Girls!" The lady from the casting with the scar down her neck was calling them from the door of the conference room.

"If you would all like to make your way in here, please! Training is about to begin!"

They filed in and sat in rows of chairs facing a small stage and a podium. At the podium there was a man who had not been at the casting.

"Ladies." He announced, "Ladies."

His voice was not very loud and yet there was a power behind it, a kind of gravitas, and also his appearance itself was striking, mesmerising in a way. He had a strange bowl haircut and a ferrety face. Creepy, thought Ceci, and she would have communicated this thought to Nicole next to her had not a strange hush descended over all of them suddenly, exactly as if they were all collectively hypnotised.

"I am," the man cast his sharp blue eyes across the rows of girls, "the client, but I am afraid that if you think that I will be sharing the name of the brand, I'm going to disappoint you." He smiled briefly, his lips were thin and curved upwards slightly at the edges giving him a joker's smile. Ceci wondered then if it was that which made him look creepy, or partially that, at least.

The conference room was relatively spacious and certainly air-conditioned, yet with the door shut the air was thick with the over sweet tangy scent of all the perfume the girls were wearing. Under it, though, something animal, sweat and something else.

Ceci did not like the man. Nicole, nearly a head taller than all the other girls, was still thinking that she had been picked by mistake.

The man went on to say that the brand was being kept secret, even from the promo teams, as part of a calculated strategy. They would be divided into teams of five girls. Each team would have a driver, who would be their manager, and a van. For up to two weeks at a time, they would be on the road, covering every town and city in the UK. They would go out on these two-week tours multiple times during the course of a year. They would stay in hotels and go out to as many pubs and clubs as they could and give out t-shirts to all the adults, white t-shirts with a purple question mark. They would, themselves, be wearing the same t-shirt and purple jeans. Grooming was paramount, make-up had to be perfect.

The idea was to generate interest, so that people talked about the product ahead of its launch. There was, needless to say, a great deal of money, a huge amount of investment, behind the product and behind the launch and anyone who revealed the name of the product, having somehow accidentally found it out, would be dealt with harshly.

"Any questions?" the man scanned his rodent-like eyes across the room.

Harshly? Thought Ceci with a shudder. Why so extreme?

"Why do we just give the t-shirt to adults?" Asked a timid voice from the front row.

"A reasonable question." the man nodded seriously, but there was sarcasm in his tone, "Would anyone like to hazard a guess as to why we will only be targeting adults with our promotion?"

"Because the product is for adults only?" offered a different, slightly more confident voice.

"I am glad you all have brains as well as looks." The man nodded, a smirk wide on his strange face.

The Teams

After his solemn, albeit a bit scary, introductory speech, the man left the stage and the room, having wished them luck in an ominous tone. There was a nervous smattering of applause and then a chubby lady with exuberant blonde curls took his place, and the whole place seemed to let out a collective sigh of relief. The lady was friendly and enthusiastic and above all, seemed normal.

"Hi everyone, so lovely to see so many gorgeous faces before me! My name is Belinda and I'm going to be working with you on the techniques we're going to use when we approach the punters with the t-shirts."

All morning, the girls were shown exactly how they were to approach the public in the pubs and clubs and exactly what they were allowed and not allowed to say and what sort of people were their target demographic. They were taught how to answer questions, and more importantly, how to evade them.

Many of them were chosen to go up onto the stage and role play possible problems. For instant, a drunk punter in a pub insisting on knowing the name of the mysterious brand.

"That is easy peasy!" Laughed Belinda into the microphone, "You don't know the brand, so you just tell him that!"

Belinda made everyone relax with her exuberant personality and no one minded the role-playing. When Nicole was chosen, though, there was a faint gasp from the crowd. She looked so obviously more exotic and high fashion than the others.

Even Belinda commented: "You're like a beautiful gazelle!" She exclaimed, exaggerated awe in her tone.

Nicole sighed inwardly and offered a rigid smile that looked more like a grimace. On the small stage she loomed over the other, much shorter girl as they improvised from versions of the set script.

"Hi my name is Nicole, we would like to present you with the gift of this t-shirt…"

"Could you interject a bit more enthusiasm into your voice maybe, Nicole?" Cajoled Belinda.

"We really hope you wear your t-shirt with pride!" Nicole spoke louder and more forcibly. She didn't sound more enthusiastic though, she sounded as if she was trying to communicate with the hard of hearing.

Belinda's smile visibly wobbled.

"I think they may get rid of me." Nicole mumbled to Ceci as she sat back down.

"Oh, I don't think so," muttered Ceci, trying to sound reassuring, but inwardly she wondered why, if Nicole wanted this gig, she didn't just play the game.

They broke for lunch and were directed to the hotel restaurant where a lavish buffet was laid out.

"Tuck in!" Trilled Belinda gaily as she led them in, "Careful of the calories though!"

Nicole grimaced again, resisting the impulse to roll her eyes.

"Not sure how long I can put up with this woman." She muttered to Ceci as they queued for the main dishes.

"She's not so bad," Responded Ceci, who was determined not to rock the boat in any way. She wanted to get away from London and from Stuart as soon as possible. "Way better than that creepy man at the beginning!" She added.

"Huh, you're right there!" Agreed Nicole, "What was up with that? He was like the scariest speaker ever, couldn't they have found someone else?"

"He is the client, isn't he? I guess he likes to feel important and in control." Ceci shrugged, weariness already hovering over her, like a cloud.

After lunch, during which Ceci did, in fact, count the calories and Nicole didn't, because she never had to, the girls were directed back into the same conference room and Belinda appeared back at the podium to announce that now they would be meeting their teams.

"I hope," She intoned, her voice vibrating with emotion, "that you will soon become close, just like a family!"

Nicole resisted the urge to make a gagging gesture.

A clipboard appeared in Belinda's hand and she started to read from the list. Nicole hoped she would be with Ceci, just because she was, by then, familiar, but Ceci wasn't sure that Nicole was a positive influence.

As the groups of five were called, the girls were directed to gather together and 'bond.' There was nervous giggling to be heard everywhere, high-pitched effusive greetings.

"Nicole, Sammy, Emma, Ceci, Becky M!" called Belinda.

Nicole and Ceci made their way to the area which was pointed out to them and watched as the other girls approached.

The Girls and their Manager

The girls were shy with each other at first, maybe a bit wary and suspicious. It was the nature of modelling and promo work that they were often pitted against each other. They pulled their chairs round into a makeshift circle and some of them giggled and smirked self-consciously.

"Maybe we should all introduce ourselves and say a few words?" It was Sammy who spoke. She was an ungainly, slightly overweight bleached blonde with hair extensions trailing down her back and spiky fake eyelashes of the darkest shade of black ink. She was clad in a white stretchy crop top and figure-hugging white jeans over which a few inches of pink flesh bulged unbecomingly.

"I'll start, shall I?" She gave a cursory glance around the group, her eyelids droopy with the weight of the lashes, but didn't wait for the others to reply.

"I'm Sammy, I'm nineteen. I got into promo work a couple of years ago because working in a clothes shop is fucking dull and that was what I did before. I live in a flat with my mum but we don't get on, so I'd like to find a bloke and move out, if you know what I mean."

Ceci would have liked to comment that she did know what Sammy meant, but finding a bloke and moving in with him was not necessarily all that it was cracked up to be. She didn't though. Sammy clearly enjoyed listening to the sound of her own voice and hadn't finished yet.

"Sometimes I think I should have stayed in school, do you know what I mean? When you're standing there giving out leaflets in some train station at seven in the morning and it's fucking freezing? But then I remember that I hated school and couldn't wait to leave."

Another one who talks too much, observed Ceci dryly to herself.

"Wonderful to meet you, Sammy!" Said Nicole, her voice brittle with fake brightness (Ceci groaned internally). "My name is Nicole. I am nearly nineteen and a fashion model. I do not usually do…" Nicole waved her slim arm around the peroxide blonde landscape of the conference room with a disparaging sweep. "This…whatever this is!"

"It pays well, this, at least!" Chimed in Becky, her tone earnest. "That is literally all I care about."

"There is no way your name is really Becky." Sammy turned to her with sharp, semi-hostile gaze. "What's your real name?"

Becky, to her credit did not cower, she stared back at Sammy with a wide-eyed disparaging look. "My 'real' name as you put it is Baheeja. It means happy." Her tone was determined, but she didn't sound particularly happy.

"What a lovely name!" Interjected Ceci, and Emma made to say something but was immediately drowned out by Sammy.

"Student, are you? Medicine or something geeky?" Her tone made it clear that she had no respect for Becky, regardless of what she studied.

"No, I am not a student nor am I an Indian cliché!" Her voice was measured but inside Becky bristled; this Sammy creature, she thought, was unbearable.

"Actually, I am an actress, well, I mean, I'm just starting out, going on auditions and stuff…"

"Well, you're certainly beautiful enough." Emma chimed in timidly. "Why don't you call yourself Baheeja though?"

"Because of prejudice." Becky shot Sammy a quick nasty look, "It's just easier, I haven't used that name in many years. I want to avoid any kind of negative attention when possible."

"It's sad that you are made to feel like that." Said Emma looking sad.

Sammy snorted. "What about you? Are you a student?" She adjusted her bulky frame to face Emma, not in a particularly friendly way.

"Oh no!" Emma laughed timidly revealing perfectly even but tiny white teeth, "I'm just a model, a glamour model, actually…"

There was a moment of silence whilst everyone tried not to look at Emma's boobs.

It was during that moment that Belinda walked over to them with an enormous man clad in, what resembled, black military type gear.

"This," She smiled widely, superficially, "is Ben, your manager."

Team Bonding

Ben had a ruddy tanned face and tiny dark eyes, even in the bright light of the conference room, they looked black. His gaze swept over the girls but his expression was curiously blank.

What's with the military get up? Thought Nicole.

Belinda was still talking. "We are recommending that as a team, you all head towards the pub to get to know each other. On us, of course…Ben will pay!"

"Hi Ben!" Sammy beamed widely enough for the rest of them.

Of course, thought Nicole, trying to stop herself from snorting out loud, Sammy was *that* sort of girl. The sort that brightened whenever she saw a man, the sort to fawn over any male in their path as if they were the best thing since sliced bread.

As an awkward group, they made their way out of the conference room and out of the hotel. Other 'teams' had clearly been given the same instruction to bond at the pub, as they all seemed to be heading in the same direction.

Other manager/drivers looked friendlier than Ben, Ceci observed, they were laughing and joking with their teams. Ben looked sombre and grim, even with Sammy walking next to him and chatting relentlessly. Hopefully, he would warm up otherwise the job would be miserable. For the first time, Ceci felt a wave of doubt wash over her. Reluctance gnawed at her, and also a bit of fear. As much as she wanted, even needed, to get away from Stuart, she honestly did not like the look of Ben at all. She wanted, more than anything in that moment, to communicate her thoughts to Nicole, but of course, there, at a pub table in front of everyone, there was no opportunity.

Ben went to the bar without saying anything and returned with a couple of bottles of white wine in an ice bucket and six glasses. He had not asked them what they wanted.

Becky shifted nervously in her seat.

"Erm, I don't actually drink, sorry."

"Why's that then?" his voice was deep and gravelly and his cold dark gaze settled on Becky with an expression of hostile curiosity.

"Because I'm Muslim." Becky mumbled, her pretty face visibly reddening.

"I'll get you a juice!" Ceci declared brightly and dashed off to the bar before anyone could comment. Once there, she observed the other tables occupied by the promo teams. They seemed to be chatty and relaxed. She could hear them well as the pub was virtually empty apart from their groups and there was no music. Ceci felt a sudden urge, standing there waiting for the barman to bring the juice, to leave, to just walk out of the exit and keep going. She looked back over at their table. She could clearly see Becky's small face wearing a fixed, unnatural smile, Nicole sporting her usual impassive expression and Emma who looked unaccountably afraid.

What was she scared of? Did she get the same feeling that Ceci did?

Ben had his back to the bar, but as Ceci watched, he got up and headed to the toilets at the back, briskly as if in need.

Ceci returned to the table with the juice.

"What a nightmare!" mumbled Emma, her lips wobbling, she looked pale and seemed close to tears.

"I know right? We've been so unfortunate with our manager allocation!" Becky nodded, "He doesn't like me, that's obvious."

"Bloody hell, you lot, give him a chance, he'll warm up! I've met his sort before." Sammy tossed her extensions over her shoulder dismissively.

"I'm sure you have." Nicole rolled her eyes.

Sammy ignored her: "Sure, the strong silent type!"

"I think that's supposed to be a positive stereotype," commented Ceci, "I'm not sure that…"

"Shhh! He's coming!" Becky hissed.

Weirdly, Ben returned from the toilet with a wide smile on his face and a complete attitude change. It was very odd. Had he chatted to someone enroute who had told him to make an effort? It was never made clear.

For the following hour, he chatted in a normal sort of way with the girls, asking them about themselves with apparent interest. He even joked about some job that he'd had before where he got locked in the toilet and couldn't get out. He went to buy them another bottle of wine, another juice for Becky and a couple of whisky chasers for himself. They stayed there until the lights came on in the pub and dusk fell outside and then all the girls made their excuses and left, except for Sammy.

They left her leaning towards Ben and giggling and chirping in a high girlish voice.

"There's nothing we can do about her." Remarked Nicole drily when they were outside. "I'm out of here. See you ladies soon!"

Sammy

Sammy wanted Ben to invite her back to his. She presumed he had some fancy bachelor pad somewhere. However, as much as she leaned towards him, enticing him with her cleavage and making unsubtle suggestive remarks, there was no invitation forthcoming.

He acted indifferent towards her, if anything. Then, outside the pub, he made it clear that he was going home alone. Had Sammy been more sensitive, she would have been offended, but as it was, as she was, she just dusted herself off and made her own drunken way home; dejected but ever-optimistic that something, *someone* else, would come up.

Also, they would all be thrown together for weeks on end on these promo tours; anything could happen!

Ever since she had heard from her agency that she had got this job, Sammy had been on cloud nine. Her agency couldn't believe it either. They were always on the point of getting rid of her because of 'being too tarty round clients.' They never, in a million years, would have expected her to get a job of this calibre involving this amount of money. In fact, the only work that had come her way since she had started promo work had been the lowliest form of leafleting, often at some provincial station during some unsociable timeslot.

Leafleting, in fact, was the bread and butter of that particular promotion agency. It was about as far from fashion modelling as it was possible to get. They had sent girls to the casting almost as a bit of a laugh. When the call had arrived citing Sammy's name, along with a few others, as having been successful, the booker had been so stunned that she had lapsed into silence on the phone. Her colleague had presumed that she was in the process of receiving bad news about her family, and was shocked to see the wide grin erupt suddenly onto her face.

Afterwards, the two women had shrieked at each other in a kind of bemused hysteria. "Sammy! Sammy? *Sammy??* No way!"

Did Sammy realise that people had such a derogatory opinion of her? Did she behave the way she did because she already had a bad reputation? Which came first, the chicken or the egg? It was never made clear, not to others.

Deep down, however, Sammy knew what had made her what she was.

That evening, she made her way slowly back to the flat she shared with her mum. She really didn't want to go home, she never wanted to go home, and, exactly as she always did, she tried to think of other places she could go, other people she could perhaps meet up with for a drink. Sammy carried, in her handbag at all times, a little address book scrawled full of telephone numbers of men, in the main, who she had been with at one time or other, usually just for the night, or more often, just for the hour.

Often, on the way back from a night out, alone, she would flip through the address book in a stinking public phone booth, teetering clumsily on her heels, smearing her make-up against the already murky glass. Who should she phone? Rarely did anyone pick up the call, (many of the numbers were, most likely, fake), and it was even rarer that anyone would agree to meet her.

That night though, she didn't fish the desperate little book out of her bag. Suddenly, Sammy felt an intense exhaustion trickle through her. She had been so elated ever since she had been informed by her baffled booker that she had got this job, and yet now, finally, she felt herself deflate.

Sammy travelled home. It took a while, especially the long walk through the poorly lit estate where she and her mother lived. Fortunately, it was summer, and even late in the evening the gloaming seemed to linger; an appealing pinkish darkness speckled with glittering stars and oftentimes illegal fireworks and lethal firecrackers which blasted through the night just like gunfire. Sammy knew they sounded like gunfire because everyone on the estate knew, unfortunately, exactly what gunfire sounded like.

Sammy and her mother lived, and had always lived, on one of the worst, the most dangerous estates in London. She unlocked the door to their flat, sober by then, or mostly sober, and immediately, just like Nicole in a different part of London, turned to wrangle the necessary, heavy bolts into place.

The worst danger for Sammy as a child, however, had not come from outside the flat, but from within.

The Big Day

It was a beautiful afternoon in August when all the girls gathered to depart on their first mystery promo tour. Since they didn't know the name of the product, that was how they had been told to refer to the job.

Each clutching a small suitcase as instructed, and wearing a freshly ironed white t-shirt with a big purple question mark front and back, as well as tight purple jeans and purple and white trainers, they gathered in an enormous, litter strewn, car park in South London under a sweltering sun.

"An inauspicious start." Muttered Nicole to Ceci, kicking cans out of her way, as the two of them approached the row of sparkling, brand new, people carriers, each painted white, of course, with the purple question mark prominently emblazoned on every feasible surface. Up close, it was apparent that the question marks were large stickers.

Ceci's stomach was already bloating against the tight waist band of the jeans and she was wondering how soon she would be able to discretely undo the top button and cover her stomach with the oversized t-shirt.

The directive was to keep the t-shirt tucked in to the jeans at all times, but surely, Ceci reasoned, that wouldn't matter whilst they were all just sitting in the van being driven to the various towns, when there was no member of the public to see them?

The girls all gathered in their teams with their manager in front of the people carriers. The managers, too, were now wearing the same clothes as the girls. It didn't really suit any of them, but it suited Ben least of all. It was the colour in particular, thought Emma, who was of artistic persuasion. He suited black, it matched his eyes and most likely his soul, she thought cynically, but kept that thought to herself.

Probably, she could have shared with Becky, the two seemed to have the beginnings of a friendship, but they weren't, Emma reasoned, close enough yet. They were standing next to each other then, they were of a similar size and height. They kind of looked as if they matched. Subconsciously, there was already a potential bond. Ceci and Nicole were conferring together behind them, muttering and Ceci occasionally sighing. Sammy was standing near them but on her own with her cheap pink plastic suitcase between her legs. The jeans were far too tight on her. The girls had been able to request their own sizes, and every single person who saw Sammy wondered why she hadn't requested the next size up. Ceci definitely would have had she not been sure that they would have been way too long in the leg.

"What is wrong with your stomach anyway?" asked Nicole then.

"I have no idea. It just gets really bloated and crampy. The doctor says it may be something I eat, but we can't figure out what."

At that moment, a hush descended over the assembled crowd and the cold-eyed client suddenly appeared in a space on the asphalt before them. He was accompanied by Belinda and the casting lady with a scar on her neck. Without a podium and in that huge space, they looked much smaller and somehow weaker and more ineffectual. Belinda spoke first, a corny little speech about maintaining pride in their appearance at all times and remembering the importance of work ethic. She tossed her curls around, conscious of how they glinted prettily in the sunlight.

"Have fun ladies! You're brilliant, you're beautiful, you deserve it!" Belinda trilled, her white teeth gleaming widely in the grey car park.

The sinister client then said a few dry words reminding them to be loyal to the brand, even if they did not know what it was yet, and to always listen to their manager. At that, he seemed to look around and catch the eye of each manager individually.

"That's fucking weird," whispered Nicole.

The casting lady just shouted 'Good Luck!' It sounded, thought Ceci gloomily, like a warning.

Emma suddenly, apropos to nothing, remembered a poem they had studied at school called 'Not waving but drowning.'

The memory appeared as a flash and then vanished.

All the girls climbed into their respective vans with their team manager behind the wheel and one by one they drove out of the car park.

They were off.

Emma

Emma, as a child had loved drawing and painting, and then, as time progressed, absolutely anything to do with arts and crafts.

From an early age, she was obsessed with colours, in particular with shades of blue. She grew up in a village near to the coast in Dorset with her parents and brother, and her favourite hobby in the world was painting seascapes, blending, and merging the colours to match the multitudinous shades of the sea. At all times, she wandered about with a palette on which blues and greys and whites swilled together in a kind of harmonious mess.

It was only a hobby, however, and that was always tacitly understood, as her parents were insistent that Emma should have a proper job, preferably some kind of trade. This was because, albeit exceptionally sensitive, she was not a studious child, so anything academic was pretty much off the table.

They were a diligent family, 'of good working-class stock,' Emma's father was fond of repeating, and Emma's parents and, as he got older, Emma's brother too, saw honour in it; the mantra of earning an honest wage for an honest day's work. Her dad and, later, her brother worked as fishermen. They endured long, brutal, wind-battered days out at sea. Emma's mum worked as a cook in various schools in the area and then at a nursing home.

When Emma had been at high school, her mum had been a dinner lady there which had been mortifying for Emma; not because she was ashamed of her mum, but because the relentless teasing which transpired because of it, made her the unhappy centre of attention.

Emma's mum was a large lady, with ruddy skin and plain of face whilst Emma herself was tiny, bespectacled, and mousey as a young teen. It was only much later that she grew the breasts which would make her money in London. It was only much later that she bleached her hair.

In her village in Dorset, no one would have ever believed it, had they been told. Her parents wouldn't have believed it either; the transformation that would unfold, that she would inflict on herself, once the tiny village persona had been cast off. In the village, she had the reputation of being shy and a reclusive homebody. She always preferred to stay quietly in her bedroom.

Her family thought she was reading romance novels and painting, and she was, but mainly, she was worrying and suffering.

Emma had realised long ago that she didn't fit in. She felt weirdly detached from the world around her, as if she had no place in it, or as if the place she had in it was merely an act; a construct of smoke and mirrors. This feeling was particularly galling around her family. She wondered, logically enough, why she didn't feel as if she belonged in the one place she was meant to, at home.

Emma, once in London, never told her family the truth. They still didn't know anything beyond the fact that she no longer wore glasses and that she was now blonde. Periodically, at Christmas and for birthdays, she would get the train to Dorset and visit them and tell lies about how she spent her days and earned her money in London.

Emma had told them that she was waitressing in London, silver service gigs, she said. She figured that it was easier that way, rather than say she was working at a particular place, a restaurant, say. That would have been much easier to check. Emma lived in fear of her parents just suddenly turning up to visit their daughter, of walking unannounced into her rented room and seeing her topless pictures lying around everywhere, her modelling portfolio thick with uncensored images of her boobs.

 Pinned to the dirty walls in her flat share, there were still watercolour seascapes too, in shades of blues and greys, the water angry and swirling. In the rundown flat they shared, her flatmates, two male gay actors (not a couple), would tell her repeatedly that she was talented, but also silently agreed that it was not enough.

They did not judge her for the glamour modelling although they did find it vaguely distasteful. They told her they worried for her, what with all the creepy photographers and her so small and literally exposed.

This job was great news for everyone though. Emma did not have to lie about it to her parents and the flatmates were happy because all three of them were behind on their rent.

Emma did not like the look of Ben, but except for Sammy, she hoped that all the girls were in the same boat and there was, in that, a kind of comforting kinship, a camaraderie.

She did not yet worry that things would get worse for all of them, that this job would be her undoing.

The First Promo Tour

The music was blaring out of speakers hidden everywhere in the interior of the van. It was Ben's choice, rock music heavy on the guitar solos, but no matter. The sun with glinting prettily through the pristine windows of the van and warming the faces of the girls. Sammy's make-up, which was, of course, too heavy, started to melt. Despite all their various reservations, there was a feeling of excitement, of anticipation, of setting of on an adventure or a holiday. The van smelt brand new, because it was brand new and none of them had ever before been in such an expensive car before. There was something vaguely intoxicating about it; about the reckless wealth it suggested that they were now, somehow, affiliated with.

There was no logic to it, they knew in the shadowy areas of their hearts that they were just minions, but the irrational elation persisted.

Ceci, strategically sitting next to Nicole in the row closest to the boot, undid the top button of her jeans and most of the zip whilst letting her t-shirt cover the transgression. Immediately, she felt relief. Her belly, escaping its rigid confines, relaxed and ballooned out. She was very glad to have got away from Stuart, it really did feel like a holiday for her. She couldn't afford to leave him and find a place of her own yet, but she had worked out that she would be able to after they had been paid for this first two-week tour.

Nicole, staring out at the landscape, (which was speeding by nearly in a blur because Ben was driving too fast), was planning how she could use the money to pay for a proper carer to come in on a daily basis and help her mother.

Sitting in the row behind Ben were Becky, Emma, and Sammy. Ben had not offered the vacant and wide passenger seat next to him to anyone and nobody had coveted it. Not even Sammy. Hungover and apparently lost in her own thoughts staring out of the window, she was being far quieter than the others would have expected.

Becky and Emma chatted in low voices amongst themselves. Because Emma's flatmates were actors and she had often socialised with them in the past, Emma found that, she and Becky knew a lot of the same people and frequented some of the same pubs.

"Does it bother you, people drinking around you when you don't?" She asked Becky.

"Ah, no, not at all, I am totally used to it. Most people are fine with it and don't even comment."

Emma glanced up quickly at the rear-view mirror to see if Ben had heard the remark and was disconcerted to observe that he appeared to be staring at her. Involuntarily, she felt heat rise to her cheeks and self-consciously she shifted, so that she was out of range of the mirror. Becky, who hadn't noticed, nudged her giggling.

"Look at Sammy!"

Despite the pounding rock music, Sammy had somehow fallen asleep, her head tipped back against the cushioned headrest, her fleshy white neck exposed and her mouth partially open and wet with drool.

"Oh no!" Emma grinned, "We shouldn't laugh, it's cruel!"

"Yeah, you're right, she is pretty mean though!" Becky shrugged.

"She is." Emma nodded, pensive suddenly, "You must get sick of people making semi-racist comments?"

"That's exactly it, the roundabout racist stuff, it's somehow worse. It's as if they don't have the guts to just come out and say what they think, but it's perfectly clear that they think it anyway. I can kind of cope with it, mainly I just ignore it, my dad not so much."

"What do you mean?" Asked Emma.

Becky explained.

Becky

From the very moment Becky's parents, Imran and Aisha had touched down at Heathrow, a year and a half before Becky and her younger sister were even born, they had wanted nothing more than to fit in.

They were young, both doctors, both having just graduated in medicine from the University of Calcutta. Initially, they lodged with some friends of friends in Ealing, whilst they searched for work. It was a tiny flat, almost shocking in its smallness.

Aisha was of a more stoic disposition, but Imran was sensitive, given to mood swings which were dependant on the weather. It was clear from the start that the colourless, damp skies in the UK did not agree with him.

They made him sad.

There was no going back, however. Their emigration was considered adventurous but also somehow inevitable. The UK offered high wages, an excellent education system and was crying out for medical professionals. They would be stupid, they knew, not to stay there; they were perfect candidates.

Furthermore, it had taken so long to manage the absurd amounts of bureaucracy and paperwork involved in moving to the UK, that really, it would be foolish to have gone through all that just to move back again to India.

That was what Aisha told Imran repeatedly during the first year, when he sulked, which was often. She had managed to get a job as a GP pretty much immediately, whereas, he was looking for a hospital position which was harder to come by.

"You'll feel better when you're working," She told him, "You have too much time on your hands to think at the moment."

"Too much time and not enough space!" He responded grimacing. They were still, at the time, lodging with the friends and cramped in the tiny flat, where damp mushroomed in the corners of their room like a sinister invading army. Imran, from a wealthy family and a huge comfortable childhood home, experienced the physical discomfort as a personal affront.

"When I think…" he would start one his laments, "about all the space I used to have…"

"You need to stop living in the past, we are here now, we must make the most of it! We can't be living with our parents forever! You know this!" Responded Aisha, exasperated and exhausted by the stress of always having to be the buoyant, optimistic one.

The same week that Aisha found out she was pregnant with Becky, Imran got a job at Hammersmith hospital as a registrar.

A week later they rented their own tiny flat in Ealing. It was just as cramped but at least there was only the two of them in it, and there was no damp.

As the years passed and their small family prospered and moved gradually to a much larger abode, Imran grew somewhat resigned to the miserable climate of his new homeland. Never a gregarious man, he made a few friends amongst colleagues at the hospital and that was enough for him.

Aisha worked part-time as a GP when the girls were small and then fully immersed herself in her profession again once they both entered high school.

It was crystal clear from an early age, that neither 'Becky' (Baheeja), nor Aalia, her sister, were cut out to be doctors. Becky (she insisted on being called that from high school onwards), confidently claimed she wanted to be an actress from the very first time she was cast as a wise man in the school nativity play.

Naturally, both of her parents were convinced that it was just a childish whim. However, as the years passed by and Becky pestered them to be allowed to join any drama group in the area and then, later on, unsuccessfully petitioned to go to a high school which specialised in performing arts, they resigned themselves to the fact that she was never willingly going to give up on the idea of acting.

To that end, Becky completed A-levels in Drama, English and Media and was, at the time of the promo job, living at home and attending auditions in London for acting jobs. She had, to date, managed to score a couple of background roles in commercials.

Becky's parents, perhaps unusually for Indian parents, understood that medicine, or even academia, was not for everyone and couldn't be forced.

Imran, in particular, always the sensitive soul, just wanted his girls to be happy and to stay close. Never a particularly happy person, he took every ignorant racist slight personally.

Given the choice, he would have liked to keep his family isolated from all the racist idiots everywhere, but of course, he couldn't do that, so instead he worried every time they left the house.

The Fancy Hotel

Ben had been silent on the two-hour drive to the first town, just intermittently fiddling with the car stereo. Because the car was huge and he was alone in the front, the girls felt almost as if they were disconnected from him in a way.

It was not a bad feeling. Emma, in particular, shuddered involuntarily whenever she looked at him. She recalled the hungry look in his black eyes when he had searched her out in the mirror and she felt all her muscles clench, like an animal on high alert.

Periodically, Ben had stopped the car, without commenting, at service stations and dashed off to the toilet.

"It seems he has a weak bladder." Remarked Becky innocently.

"Hmm…" Muttered Nicole. "There's definitely something wrong with him, not sure it's that though."

Sammy woke up suddenly with a jerk as they were passing Birmingham. She swore loudly and fished a hand mirror out of a white plastic handbag on her lap.

"Why didn't any of you tell me I was drooling?" She turned to face Becky and Emma scowling.

"We didn't notice!" commented Becky in a mock- innocent tone, nudging Emma and trying not to giggle.

Sammy swore again, under her breath, and spent the remainder of the drive padding ineffectually at her sweaty face with a powder puff.

Mid-afternoon, they pulled into the car park of a very fancy-looking hotel. It was just on the outskirts of the town they would be working in for a while.

"This will be your home for the next four days!" Announced Ben as he switched off the engine and the girls startled at the unexpected sound of his voice shattering the stillness where the relentless rock music had been. Then they all stared at the entrance to the hotel and almost simultaneously exclaimed:

"WOW!"

It was situated at the edge of a decorative park and doubled as a Spa hotel. The building was elaborately designed to look like a castle, possibly to endow it with mystique and glamour. It certainly impressed the five girls, few of whom had ever stayed in a hotel, and none of them in one as fancy as this.

"Some ground rules." Ben loomed over them just as they were about to enter the main door. "Room allocations are as follows: Cecilia, Nicole, and Sammy together in one room and then, Becky and Emma in another. Breakfast and dinner are included and you are allowed to use the pool and the gym, but under no circumstances are you allowed to take anything from the mini bar or drink alcohol at all unless you are with me, neither in this hotel nor elsewhere. Some of the staff here know me and they *will* report to me if they notice any transgressions! All clear so far?"

He ran his dark gaze over all of them, and it seemed to Emma, that it lingered on her face. She tried to shuffle behind Nicole.

They all nodded and mumbled assent.

"So, I will meet you all, every night, either downstairs or at the van, at exactly 7.30 on each night in each location. You will be dressed and ready to go. I will have your bags of t-shirts to distribute, you just need to make sure that you look as perfect as you can."

Ben smirked as he said that, it was unmistakable. The girls weren't really listening though. As he was speaking, an excited and very exuberant Hen party was making its way past them and into the lobby.

Must be brilliant, they all thought, with no small amount of envy, to just be there to have fun with your friends.

The Hotel Rooms

Their allocated rooms were next to each other on the second floor, but nowhere near Ben's, as far as they knew. Emma, nevertheless, peered fearfully behind her, as the girls manoeuvred their bags down the carpeted, synthetic-smelling hallway towards their rooms. He hadn't, as far as she was aware, come up behind them in the lift, not to the second floor anyway. She let out a sigh of relief.

They had only been given one key per room which was not an issue for Becky and Emma, but Nicole and Sammy were already squabbling and they hadn't even seen the room yet.

The sterile anonymity of the big chain hotel room enchanted all the girls, impressed them even. All the absolute necessities of comfort and hygiene in compact form, condensed. The neatness of it alone was charming. But, of course, they knew the cost of it too. Knew that the price was prohibitive for their own families, and there was an elation that came from that. They did not care that all the rooms looked the same, that the furnishings were grey and bland, that their rooms overlooked the car park and not the park.

They had a clear view of the white people carrier emblazoned with purple question marks. It seemed to be sitting there waiting for them like a slavish dog.

That was what Ceci thought as she looked out of the window, trying to ignore the row that was unfolding behind her. Nicole and Sammy were arguing about who should get the 'extra' fold out bed.

"I am bigger than you!" Sammy hissed at Nicole, the make-up orange and blotchy on her face.

"You may be bigger but I am taller!" laughed Nicole. "I need the leg room of the normal bed."

She was confident that she would win the argument, thought Ceci, that is why she treated it as a joke. There was a toughness to Nicole which was intimidating if you crossed her. It was as if a shutter came down and eradicated the amenability, nothing but fight was left. Ceci could see a glimmer of it only then, but intrinsically knew that it could get worse.

Sammy, whether intimidated or not, it was hard to tell, backed down and took the camp bed.

Neither her dark mood nor Nicole's could withstand that initial holiday-like excitement, however. They had been told that they could wear their own clothes when they were not working and Ceci called Becky and Emma's room and they all arranged to meet at the gym.

"Next time we should bring costumes for the pool!" Ceci laughed as they headed down the stairs in order to get there quicker. They were wearing leggings and t-shirts, Sammy's was a crop top, as usual.

"Why is this girl obsessed with showing her tummy?" Whispered Emma.

"Don't be mean!" Giggled Becky.

"Do you think that all the hotels will be like this?"

"Probably, I guess the advertising agency has some kind of deal with this chain, so they will probably all be similar."

"Oh wow, this job will be like an extended holiday!"

"Steady on, we haven't done anything yet, it might be hideous and Ben, well, I don't trust him."

They were all, by then, in the hotel gym. It was not large, but it looked brand new, it had the same synthetic new plastic smell as the car, and they were the only people in it. They were sprawled out on the mats stretching. Nicole was instructing them, because, she informed them, she had been very sporty as a kid and knew what she was doing. There was giggling, it was fun.

Still, at the mention of Ben, they all looked around, as if he may have been hiding somewhere and spying on them.

"He's weird, but hopefully, he'll just leave us alone during the days."

"He's more than weird, he's creepy."

"I think he's kind of bipolar, one minute he's all friendly, the next, there's this blank look on his face and he's totally hostile."

"He's not as bad as that client!"

"I don't know." It was Emma speaking in a low voice. "I have this bad feeling that they are all in cahoots."

"Don't be silly!" Becky, who was sitting cross-legged next to her, placed one slim arm around her shoulders, "That's paranoia talking! There's five of us remember, and only one of him, Ben, I mean, and the creepy client is miles away!"

Instinctively, Ceci glanced towards Nicole. There may have been five of them, but it was Nicole who would protect them, she thought, if they ever needed it.

The First Night on the job

The girls all took turns to have showers after the gym, and then had great fun ordering room service, a new experience for all of them. Then they got dressed for work, and jostled in front of the mirrors doing their make-up.

They were downstairs, spic and span and ready for work five minutes early.

"Has anyone else noticed how people are staring at me?" Muttered Becky as they waited.

"They're looking at me too," Commented Nicole in a dismissive tone, "They are not used to brown-skinned people."

"Doesn't it bother you?"

"Not really, any time I've been out of London, it's the same. Also, what would be the point of getting bothered by it?"

"Well, I hate it." Commented Becky. "Except for when I am acting, I don't want people staring at me."

Ben appeared just then, wearing the same uniform. The girls wondered if he had been napping whilst wearing it; he looked creased and ruffled and a bit bedraggled.

He clearly wasn't in a happy mood.

"Right then," he instructed in a tired voice, "Let's get this show on the road, off you go, into the van." He handed them each a voluminous purple shoulder bag stuffed full of t-shirts, all rolled up in small bundles. They were easier to hand out that way, the girls had been told.

Back in the van and the rock music went on again, louder this time, it seemed to rebound within their heads. The girls nudged each other or pressed their leg against that of their neighbour, each comforted by the presence of the others. Even Sammy, by then, had been accepted into the fold; maybe not entirely, but certainly partially and more than before.

Ben sped along the dull provincial roads leading into the town and then pulled up with a screech in front of an uninspiring-looking pub.

Before he unlocked the van doors, (Emma had already noticed, unhappily, that Ben had exclusive control of the locks), Ben turned to face them all and told them that this wasn't really their target demographic, but they were here so that the girls could warm up and have a quick practice of what they had learnt at training.

The doors of the van unlocked with a loud metallic clicking sound.

"Only half an hour here, set your watches, off you go!"

The girls jumped out of the van exchanging anxious glances.

"Right, let's get on with it!" Nicole said in a determined voice, and relieved that someone was taking charge, the others stepped into line behind her and followed her lead.

Inside, it was relatively empty but Nicole headed straight over to a table of young men and started her spiel. Her voice wavered a bit and the men looked bemused until they realised that they were getting something for free.

"What's the catch love?"

"No catch, honest."

"You are gorgeous, we don't often get your type in these parts!"

"Erm, thanks." Nicole plastered a fixed grin onto her face, she knew her jaw would be aching by the end of the night.

The other girls watched her for a minute or so and then, with varying degrees of nervousness, spread out and approached the clusters of drinkers. There were quite a lot of old men, who were certainly not within the target demographic, but, flustered as they were, the girls approached them anyway and they were delighted with their t-shirts. They proffered amused, yellow-toothed grins.

During the training day, it had been made repeatedly clear that their manager would always stay in the pubs with them in case of a problem, but Ben had stayed in the van. Exactly half an hour later the girls emerged from the pub to find him smoking in the driving seat with the door open, his music echoing across the car park.

"How did it go?" He asked. He was grinning widely, clearly in a much better mood.

"You were right, it was good practice." Nicole commented, and the others nodded their heads in agreement. They felt the temporary elation of having completed a job they were anxious about for the first time. It was nerve-wracking, not because it was a difficult job, but because it was the best paid gig that any of them had ever had, and they didn't want to jeopardise it.

The Job

For the rest of that night and during the subsequent nights in that town, the job became routine until the girls found that they were reciting their lines automatically. They quickly noticed that Ben never came into the pubs and clubs with them, which meant that, as no one was watching, they were less careful about who they approached and often gave away the t-shirts recklessly, without the proper protocol, to those who were too young or too old.

As a rule, they were relieved he wasn't there to supervise, but sometimes in the packed, slightly rougher bars, it would have been useful to have a 'protector.' It was Nicole and Becky who mostly seemed to fall prey to leering drunken men with their innuendoes and supposedly ambiguous racist remarks. Sammy, too, suffered from her fair share of abuse, a great deal of groping in her case.

"Why the hell is Ben not in here with us, protecting us?" Complained a disgruntled Sammy, shouting over the loud music in the club they were in. Some guy had just grabbed her bum and refused to let go.

"I have a theory about that." Commented Nicole grimly.

"You and your theories!" Sammy rolled her eyes. While she seemed to get on better with the others superficially, she had little time for what she called their 'conspiracy theories' about Ben and the client. Mainly, she was annoyed that repeat exposure to her charms had still not managed to entice Ben.

Nevertheless, all the girls, including Sammy, almost always hung out together during the day, having established, right from the start, a sort of routine which would only ever differ slightly from town to town in the months to come: Sleeping in, a hotel breakfast, usually in the restaurant, occasionally room service. A walk to the, often forlorn-looking, town and a mooch around the shops with a lot of disparaging remarks about how rubbish they were compared to London. Maybe a nap in the afternoon or a film on TV, sometimes the gym (in other towns, later, the pool), a shower, a room service dinner and work.

That routine was adhered to, more or less, despite the other things that started happening. There was comfort in it, there is always comfort in routines and as time passed, they would come to rely on any comfort they could get.

On that first tour, the girls had almost nothing to do with Ben.

"He's not a manager at all, he's just a driver. Literally all he does is drive us to the venues!" Commented Nicole, "Seriously, he must get big money for this, for effectively doing nothing."

"What are you going to do about it? Complain to the client?"

"We should!" That was Emma. Although nothing had happened, she was afraid of him, almost subconsciously. It was as if her body knew to be afraid. Whenever he so much as glanced at her, the hair on the back of her neck stood up, all her muscles tensed.

"I wouldn't," Ceci shuddered, "We would get someone worse instead, as a punishment."

"I don't know, the other managers looked better, more friendly."

"We wouldn't get those men though, would we? They are taken! We would be sent some random creep." Ceci tried and failed to keep the sarcasm out of her voice.

Ceci was in a bad mood anyway. Stuart had taken to calling the hotel. The worst thing about that was that she had never given him the name of the hotel, just the names of the towns on the tour, because he had insisted with his annoying petulant voice. He had rung around all the hotels in town until he had found her. When the phone had rung in their room, she had presumed it was the other girls. They were always calling each other.

"Found you." Said Stuart, and Ceci had felt her stomach dip and cramp.

Four nights in the first place and then they packed their bags, Ben checked them out and they drove on to the second town, an hour away.

The rock music was becoming familiar; the girls started to recognise the songs rebounding in their heads. At night sometimes, the lyrics would come to them, lines here and there embedded in their dreams.

First Tour, Second Town

"We're like pop stars with a tour bus." Commented Sammy. "Soon we will have no clue what town we're in on any given night!"

"I think pop stars get more help from their manager than we do." Nicole muttered sourly. "Probably have more fun and get more money too."

The same room allocation, and she had reluctantly agreed to take the fold out bed this time.

"Don't worry, my boyfriend will track me down and tell us where we are," Ceci sighed grimly. "he'll always know which town we're in."

That hotel was part of the same chain, as predicted, but this time, their rooms had a view of a river.

"It's a canal, I think, too narrow for a river." Emma was leaning out of the window, her arms dappled pleasantly in the heat of the sun shining through the trees. She had been relieved to observe that, once again, Ben's room was somewhere else, in another part of hotel, another floor.

"Do you think all the hotels we stay in are this big?" She asked Becky hopefully.

"Probably, if they're all part of the same chain."

Becky didn't really know, but, by then, she felt almost as if she could read Emma's mind, they had become very close very quickly. Maybe because there was just the two of them in the room, they spent a lot of time talking deep into the night.

The group had arrived early afternoon, and the girls decided to go for a walk to explore. They had left Ben sitting at the hotel bar, beer, and cigarette in hand. He had watched them leave without smiling. Sammy had raised her hand in a friendly salute but he had ignored her.

The route to town was through an attractive flower filled park.

"I think this town may be a bit more upmarket." observed Ceci.

"Don't worry," muttered Nicole, "I'm sure we'll get to visit the grottiest pubs though!"

"That's not fair." Sammy was trailing along behind them. Whilst travelling from one town to another, Ben had told them they were allowed to wear their own clothes. Under the glaring summer sun, Sammy was, predictably enough, wearing hot pants and a cropped black vest top which resembled a bikini top more than anything else.

"None of the venues have been that bad, not really!"

"We all know the type of venues she's used to!" Nicole mumbled under her breath to Ceci.

Ceci wasn't listening. She was wondering when Stuart would phone. It was a matter of when not if, she knew. The last time he had kept her on the line for an hour with his paranoia and baseless accusations. His voice had been so loud that it could be heard clearly in the hotel room even though Ceci had kept the receiver rammed against her ear.

Both Nicole and Sammy had pretended not to listen, but afterwards, when Sammy was in the bathroom, Nicole had sat down opposite Ceci who was slumped on the bed, looking dejected.

"What the hell does he think it is that you're doing?"

"Flirting with people in the pubs, finding his replacement, talking to men…"

Ceci sighed deeply.

"Have you explained to him what most of these people are actually like?" Nicole pictured, as she spoke, the toothless men with their nicotine-stained fingers and dirty fingernails.

"It wouldn't even matter if he saw them!" Ceci laughed bitterly, "He's obsessed, it's a control thing."

"Less than a week and a half to go though and then you can take the money and run, eh?"

"What's that?" Sammy emerged from the bathroom. "Hell, no! Whatever you do, you shouldn't leave one man before you find the next!"

"She's not like you!" Nicole scoffed, "Doesn't *need* a man! She's not desperate!"

"Are you calling me desperate?" Sammy had a white fluffy towel wrapped around her, her extensions pulled up in a high pony tail on top of her head. Without make-up, she had no eyebrows or eyelashes. She looked strangely blank.

"If the cap fits…" muttered Nicole.

Town to be Blamed

On the second last night in that town, in the van on the way out to the pubs, Ben suddenly turned the rock music all the way down.

"When we get back to the hotel tonight, we should go for a drink." He was still driving, his tone matter-of-fact. It wasn't a question. Emma noticed that maybe more than the others did, it was a demand.

"Great!" enthused Sammy.

The others didn't respond and, wary of the mirror, didn't change the expressions on their faces, but imperceptibly, they leaned into each other, an unspoken solidarity.

That entire evening, while she worked, Emma was haunted by the colours of the sea, the multitudinous shades of blue and grey. Standing there in various pubs like a robot handing out t-shirts on autopilot, she felt suddenly as if she was desperate to paint, she felt compelled, as if it would save her somehow, from what, she wasn't completely sure. In her nightmares, it was Ben who came at her with his colossal frame, his eyes glinting with a black nothingness.

That very morning, hanging in the hotel restaurant, Emma had noticed, not a seascape, but a painting of, what was presumably, the waterway outside their window. The predominant colours had been a dark metallic grey, a liquid black. The river seemed, about all else, profound, and sinister, although the sky above it was incongruously bright turquoise.

Once back in their room, Emma found that the painting had ruined her perception of the river. Now, when she leant out of the window to gaze at it, it terrified her. Emma tried to explain this to Becky, but she had just looked perplexed.

"I think you are over-thinking it." She furrowed her brow and dragged a brush through her thick hair. "It's just a painting, and that," She gestured outside their window, "Is just a river or a canal, you know what I mean."

That evening when they got back to the hotel, Ben told them he would meet them at the hotel bar in half an hour and he himself headed straight there. Sammy grabbed the room key from Nicole and made her way up the stairs excited to get ready. The others made their way slowly behind her.

"Do you think we really have to go?" Emma was desperate not to.

"Look," said Nicole evenly, her voice low, "It's strategic on our part, it shows good will. We are stuck with him and I think it is important that we try to get on, it's one drink and yet if we refuse, it looks really bad."

"What about if we just send Sammy?" laughed Becky.

"I don't think he likes her at all!" Ceci snorted.

"Who do you think he likes?" Emma whispered fearfully.

Nicole stared at her in surprise. They were in the corridor outside their rooms.

"Is that what's worrying you? You think he has his sights set on you?" She narrowed her eyes at Emma and then winked.

"Look, I know he's creepy, but I haven't seen anything that makes me afraid he's going to pounce. Don't worry! Your Auntie Nicole will protect you!"

Except for Sammy who had got changed into a figure-hugging stretchy dress, the others agreed to stay in their purple jeans. She had already got changed by the time they reluctantly made their way up stairs and dashed out again, alone, to be the first to join Ben.

"Seriously!" Laughed Nicole, "He's all yours, believe me. You won't have to fight the rest of us off!"

Ceci's stomach felt painful and bloated as it always did at the end of the night, and surreptitiously she untucked her t-shirt and undid the top button of her jeans.

"Don't worry, he won't notice, Sammy will inevitably draw all the attention, for all the wrong reasons!"

"Nicole is right, you know." Becky was saying to Emma. The two were sitting on their beds facing each other. Emma had her fists clenched. "It's actually worse if we don't go, it draws attention."

Emma nodded. She understood the logic in it, but still, her entire body bristled to stay away from him as if he was a toxic forcefield.

Just One Drink

By the time the others had reluctantly descended and joined Ben and Sammy at the hotel bar, Sammy was leaning into him, her fingers, with her long pink painted nails clutching a bottle of beer. The scene resembled, for a second, that first 'getting to know each other' session in the pub in London.

This bar was very quiet though, and dimly lit, with orange lanterns emitting a warm, flattering glow. During the day some sort of corporate conference had taken place in the hotel, there had been lots of serious people in conservative suits milling around. A few of them now remained and had gathered around a table in the corner of the bar, but apart from them it was empty.

Ben was sitting wide legged on a bar stool, facing away from the bar and towards Sammy also on a bar stool.

"Pull up a stool!" He called over to the girls, his tone unusually jovial. Was he drunk already or on something else?

"Why don't we get a table?" Suggested Nicole mildly, "It's more comfortable."

There was something about his splayed legs that seemed distasteful if not outright suggestive.

Emma, deliberately not looking at Ben, noticed for the first time, another painting of the river which was positioned to the side of the optics but also behind the bar.

In this one, the river was a dark emerald green with pale lily pads floating sporadically. The sky above it was the lightest blue grey. Emma nudged Becky who was standing close beside her.

"Look!" She indicated the picture, "I much prefer this one, what do you think?"

"Lovely, yes." Becky was distracted. Sammy had grabbed Ben's meaty, tanned forearm as she pretended to slip off the bar stool, giggling. They sat at the table. There were cushioned chairs at least and the others slumped. Ceci was worrying about her bloated tummy. Emma was deliberately distracting herself by thinking of the painting of the river and how she herself would go about portraying it.

Ben went to buy wine for them, without asking, as before.

"He already bought a beer for me." Announced Sammy with pride.

"Bless." Nicole muttered, "It's not an achievement to boast about."

White wine arrived in an ice bucket, Ben's smile arrived with it, wide and wolfish. Nicole was the least flappable of the girls, the toughest she liked to think, and yet it made her nervous, how temperamental he was, how unstable his moods and dispositions.

Cocaine, she thought to herself then, as the wine was poured, the girls drank and Ben started on a relentlessly long convoluted story about a horse racing mishap. Nicole personally had no experience of cocaine, had not seen much of it, (on the estate, it tended to be heroin, weed, speed that was sold in the main, crack in recent years,) but Ben seemed to be a text book case from all that she had been told; moody and aggressive one minute, gregarious and effusive the next.

"You're very quiet." Ben broke off suddenly, his smile vanished and he glared at them. "I don't want to be here, just talking to myself! I could do that alone in my room."

They all sat up straight, like kids being told off by a headmaster, but worse. Emma pictured immediately his room. Of course, it would be a carbon copy of theirs, bland and beige. But he would be in it, breathing heavily, like an ogre and through his window the river would run like inky syrup, pitch black.

Nicole swallowed. She had been half joking about protecting the girls and yet now she felt like the responsible one.

"Our voices get exhausted talking to the punters about t-shirts, there's so much shouting too, above the music, our throats get a bit sore, sorry."

"All the more reason to drink then! Drink up! There's more where that came from!"

Reluctantly, they drank, all except Becky who cradled her pint class of water. His mood improved again as Sammy, drunk by then, having helped herself liberally from the bottle, entertained them with stories of the more ridiculous promotions jobs she had had. Ben didn't fancy her, that much was obvious, but he liked the fact that she spoke.

"You're the most sociable one!" He raised his glass to her and she beamed.

It was past two when Ben declared that it was time for bed.

"I'll stay for another one!" Wheedled Sammy. Her hand was very close to his on the table and Ceci noticed her nail polish was chipped.

"No." His voice heavy and firm again, "That's enough now. We've a longer drive ahead of us tomorrow."

Rain

They were driving on the motorway, late in the morning, to the last destination of that tour and the rain was sluicing down. The wipers swished relentlessly, the metallic, rhythmic sound drowned out by the ubiquitous rock music. They had all managed to get drenched just getting from the hotel to the van lugging their bags, and their clothes smelt damp. The air was thick with humidity and as their wet clothes stuck to them gradually with sweat, discomfort itched at their skin.

There were hours of that. Five hours.

 Ben's countenance, from the start, had been grim and taciturn, all memories of jollity the previous night wiped clean, as if completely erased from his memory.

Just a few days more of this, before the first big payment. The girls were all calculating what they would do with the money in their heads. They could put up with just a bit more, they had each other after all. Sporadically, their eyes would lift from the contemplation of the sodden grey landscape (fields in the main), and look at each other; there was comfort in it, solidarity. More so even as time passed. The knowledge that they were not alone in this was priceless.

Ben stopped at three service stations on the way and each time he emerged from the men's toilet elated and in a better mood. He didn't speak much but he would sing along to the music in his coarse voice and his fingers would beat time on the steering week. Nicole watched him surreptitiously, out of the corner of her eye, and she estimated that the effect of whatever he was taking would wear off in approximately 45/50 mins, hence the renewed need for a service station stop.

She felt somehow that it was significant information, that it may come in useful at some point.

Occasionally, the girls would get out at the service stations too, just to use the toilet, but they always went in clusters and were careful not to watch him and not to enter the toilet area at the same time.

The weather cleared slightly as they approached the town which was their final destination, but the sky hung heavy and threatening over them, like a grey canopy, and the air felt suffocating and still. In the van it was even worse because Ben smoked continuously and, for whatever reason, he disliked the air conditioning. The girls smoked too, all except Becky, but were not allowed to do so in the van, ever.

As soon as they arrived in the car park of the hotel and Ben unlocked the doors, the girls tumbled out and stretched, taking deep ineffectual gulps of the static damp air.

"There isn't a river here, I don't think." Remarked Emma sadly.

"I didn't realise you were that attached to it!" Quipped Nicole.

"I think it's the paintings she's attached to." Muttered Becky, silently rolling her eyes. The river obsession was starting to get on her nerves.

"Never mind," She said soothingly to Emma, "There's bound to be other paintings here."

Same hotel chain, same colour décor, same routine, same room allocation. They had arrived late, five in the afternoon, sweaty and bedraggled from the long drive, they took turns having showers and ordered room service. The menu was the same as before, there was an odd comfort in the predictability of their choices, the way they now knew what the others liked to eat.

"Paintings of flowers in this hotel." Remarked Emma, standing, with a white towel wrapped around her tiny frame, in front of the oil painting in their room depicting red roses drooping out of their vase, overcrowded, their stems jostling for space.

"That's good too, right?" Remarked Becky with a touch of impatience. The obsession with paintings, too, was starting to bug her.

Emma didn't reply, reverting instead to her old fear.

"His room is not near ours, is it?"

Becky sighed, she hadn't paid attention this time.

"No, no, don't worry." She crossed her fingers.

That town was bigger. Each evening promotion shift was slightly longer as there were more drinking establishments to get to.

"A student town." Ben announced with a sneer as they climbed into the van in their uniforms, their hair still damp from the shower and fragrant with the hotel shampoo.

None of the girls were students so there was no reaction from them. The first pub was clearly full of students though, the girls in hippyish garb and lots of jewellery and clumpy boots, the boys in the same boots with long floppy hair and t-shirts featuring obscure Indie bands.

They were very friendly with the girls, curious about the promotion and super grateful for their t-shirts. The students seemed extremely bemused that the girls had no idea what they were promoting, and through their eyes the promo girls started to wonder anew.

"Are you guys with that big bloke smoking in the van?" A girl asked Ceci, "He looks scary, rather you then me!"

Yes, Ceci thought later. I wish I was you too. She had never considered university. In her family, people left school at sixteen or eighteen (at the latest) and worked. But students, Ceci imagined then, were more immune from the likes of Ben, less exposed. It was as if they were frozen in a state of childhood innocence for longer.

Hot Chocolate

It rained heavily on and off all week, and most of the places the girls visited in the evenings with their purple bags of t-shirts were exclusively the domain of students. There were dingy, damp smelling basements with skinny boys leaping and sweating in front of a makeshift stage upon which an amateur band shouted and screeched, lively pubs where the drinks were too cheap and there was no personal space, student bars which were little more than undecorated rooms with trendy graffiti and peeling posters on the walls and where the drinks were cheaper still.

The concept of being a student was enticing Ceci more and more, improbable as the prospect was for her, for people like her and yet… She wondered if the others thought about it at all. It was inevitable that they would notice how much friendlier the students were compared to the normal rough townsfolk they had to deal with, how carefree and guileless they seemed.

Very occasionally, however, a boy and his overly well-spoken group would make leery comments designed to emphasize their superiority in status, their comparative wealth.

Posh students.

"They are playing at being powerful and important like their fathers." Nicole commented later.

All five girls were gathered in 'her' room at the end of the second night. They had come across several groups of the blonde floppy-haired 'toffs' that night in various student venues and were comparing notes.

The girls had ordered hot chocolate from room service, Ceci's idea. The room smelt sickly sweet; of boiled milk and sugar. The girls felt snuggled in it somehow. There was, about it, a nostalgia for childhood, real or imagined.

"How is that different from the working men we meet with their gang of mates all making rude remarks?"

"It's not different exactly, it's two sides of the same…beast." By then they were leaning out of the wide window, smoking. Underneath them was the car park. "It just comes from a different perspective, a different place."

Ceci snorted. "The students from the rich families think that one day they will be able to own the likes of us, if not here in the UK, then our counterparts somewhere in Asia, somewhere abroad."

"We are models not hookers!" Emma's anguished small voice.

"It doesn't matter what we actually are." Nicole explained patiently, "For the purposes of this discussion, it matters how they perceive us to be! Promo girls, models, strippers, waitresses…in their eyes it's all similar and the rich don't think they need to worry about a distinction."

She threw the stub of her cigarette in the direction of their people carrier, gleaming yellowish in the orange half-light of a street lamp, the purple stickers black and peeling.

"The girls they marry would not do this job." Ceci commented into the silence that followed.

"What about the working-class men, how do you think they see us?" Becky asked. She was leaning out of the window with them, even though she didn't smoke.

"Ah Becky," Nicole chuckled, "That question impacts differently for me and you, especially in provincial towns!"

"I'm not sure that's true," Commented Ceci, "I think seeing any of us do jobs like this, and suspecting we're getting paid a lot, annoys the hell out of the working-class men. They resent women being paid more than them, I think. Sometimes, and honestly, I've seen this, even though they are chatty and thankful for the t-shirts and everything, there's a nasty feeling behind it, as if they hate us almost."

"That's stupid," Snorted Sammy, "This whole conversation is stupid. Nobody hates us! They either fancy us or they don't, it's not that deep."

"Thanks for your input, Sammy!" Nicole rolled her eyes and laughed.

From somewhere close by, they heard another laugh, a throaty, unpleasant chuckle which was unfortunately familiar to them all.

As one, the girls froze, huddled together leaning out of the window. Emma was the first to move, she gasped and toppled backwards.

"You told me he wasn't near us!" She hissed at Becky in an anguished whisper. "He's two rooms down, he was leaning out of the window, I saw him!"

Cocktails

Ben insisted on taking the girls for a drink in the hotel bar on the penultimate night. Of course, they didn't want to go, but as before, they did not see a way of getting out of it politely.

"We are so close, so close to getting our money!" Nicole muttered to Ceci whilst Sammy was in the bathroom redoing her make-up unnecessarily. Nicole didn't trust Sammy, at heart none of them did. They didn't think of her as cunning, just blundering, and foolish, and somehow a liability.

"We just have to keep our heads down for a couple more days."

"Well, more than that if we do the other tours as well, of course." Ceci commented sagely.

The two of them were sitting, still in their uniforms waiting for Sammy so that they could descend to the bar all together to meet him, as a cohesive unit.

"Strength in numbers." Emma was saying to Becky in the room next door.

"We don't need any strength, he's harmless!" Becky sighed., flopping down on her bed. She was getting increasingly intolerant of what she thought of as Emma's paranoia.

"Do you really believe that?"

"Yeah, I do!" Becky was tired after the busy night they'd had. The last thing she wanted to do was drink water in the hotel bar and smile politely at Ben, whilst also trying to stop Emma from having some kind of panic attack.

As before, all the girls stayed in their uniform apart from Sammy who had pulled on a figure hugging stretchy black dress.

"Is that really necessary?" Muttered Nicole watching her, "We are literally just going downstairs!"

"Nothing wrong with making a bit of an effort." Sammy pouted at the mirror whilst smearing on the bright, sticky lipstick she always wore.

Ceci sighed heavily.

"Come on then, let's get this over with."

They knocked next door and the other two girls joined them slouching and yawning.

"Do you think we're going to have to drink with him in every town now?" Came Emma's small voice.

"Yes." Said Nicole simply. "I know it's not ideal but to be fair to him, he hasn't been that bad so far, totally bearable."

In fact, he had been better than the cynic in Nicole had presumed he would be. It must be, she thought, dependant on how his drugs affected him at any given moment, and at which stage of the cycle he was.

Later, she would laugh bitterly at how naïve she had been there in that student town on their first tour.

On a table near to the hotel bar, he had laid out five brightly coloured cocktails, all in different rainbow hues and complete with rainbows and glace cherries. He was standing next to the display and grinning proudly like a kid presenting a science project at school.

"Your one has no alcohol in it!" He announced quickly to Becky. He gestured to a bright orange drink with a tall straw in the shape of a giraffe.

"Right." Said Becky, "Erm…thank you."

"I never would have imagined that the bar staff at this hotel would be able to make something so…exotic!" Nicole commented. She looked over at the small bar where a spotty youth, barely eighteen, was drying glasses.

"Well, I gave them some instructions, anyway, don't just stand there waiting for the ice to melt! Tuck in!"

Dutifully they sat and drank. The cocktails were very sweet, the chairs were soft and comfortable and the lights were low.

Conversation was relaxed but desultory, they all felt very tired. The night had been long and the venues they had frequented had, as always, been loud, necessitating lots of shouting.

The girls all finished their first drink and Ben hurried to the bar to get them another.

"You should all try different colours and flavours this time!" He seemed in a great mood.

"He's not drinking cocktails," Commented Emma whilst he was at the bar, "He's drinking bottled beer."

"And so?" Becky shrugged and yawned. She felt so sleepy she could barely keep her eyes open.

First Tour, Last Day

The next morning, the girls struggled to open their eyes.

"I'm absolutely exhausted." Yawned Ceci.

"Me too." Nicole stretched her long thin arms above her head and rotated her shoulders. "I feel like I've done a really long workout."

"Well, I supposed we did go to the gym yesterday."

"Are you kidding? We barely do anything at the gym, just slouch around. Last time I felt like this I had flu."

"Oh no! Do you think we are sick?"

"I don't know but thank God we're going home tomorrow!"

"Yeah, I can't wait!" Ceci exclaimed with a sleepy grin, "As soon as I get hold of that money, I'm going to show Stuart the door."

"I don't know, that could get messy, he will almost certainly refuse to go. I think you should grab your stuff and just leave, find your own place."

"That could take ages."

"In the meantime, why don't you come and stay with me and my mum? She's alright, you know, a good egg. She won't bother you, she can barely move. Honestly, we could use some help around the flat!" Nicole emitted a low irreverent chuckle.

"Really, are you sure?" Ceci perked up suddenly.

"Sure, I'm sure, now would you look at Sammy?"

Sammy was lying stretched out with the black dress she was wearing the night before scrunched up over her boobs. Her white tummy and black lace pants were visible. She had not removed her make-up the night before and the hotel pillow was smeared in beige and pink gunk.

Ceci and Nicole observed her dispassionately.

"I know how she feels," commented Ceci, "I remember struggling to wash my face, I was so tired."

Sammy groaned loudly when they tried to wake her and insisted that they leave her alone, so they gave up and went down to breakfast with Becky and Emma. They both looked exhausted too, their skin had a greyish cast.

"We were saying that maybe we were sickening for something?" said Emma.

"That's an old-fashioned expression!"

"I know, my mum used to say it a lot."

"I feel like I'm hungover but of course I don't drink and I would have been able to tell if there was alcohol in that, I think I would anyway?" Becky looked perplexed.

"Maybe not." Nicole was pensive. "Maybe the drinks were just really strong and maybe yours did have alcohol in it?"

"Anyway, I'm too tired to do anything. Honestly, I kind of feel like going back to bed."

"Yeah, same!"

"How about we hang out in our room, watch a film, and then nap after lunch?

"Like old ladies!"

"Yeah!" They grinned, helping themselves liberally to coffee in the hope that they would feel more alert and awake.

After breakfast, they all retired to the bigger room where Sammy was just emerging from slumber with a dramatic groan.

"Why is everyone here and why did you all go to breakfast without me?" She peered at them all through bloodshot eyes, her hair hanging in straggly clumps over her shoulders. Sammy always wore so much make-up that she looked slightly shocking without it, like a whole different person.

The timeslot for the hotel breakfast had, by then, passed.

"Chill, you can get room service, let's get hot chocolates again!" Ceci grabbed the phone and started dialling.

It was raining outside and the room became, as the hours passed, a stuffy, sour-smelling cocoon, but for that day, the girls felt secure, albeit weirdly dopey. Later they napped whilst watching a film, cuddled up and leaning on each other like puppies. For a brief while only Ceci and Emma were awake and the former studied the latter curiously.

"May I ask, if you don't mind, why glamour modelling? You don't seem, I don't know, it sounds rude, and I don't mean to be rude, but you don't seem the type?"

"Well, I'm too short and curvy for fashion modelling."

"Yes, but…"

"When I was a kid, I would see all the men in our town staring at the girls in the papers, the page three girls, and I thought it was glamourous, well not glamourous exactly, but something better than nothing, I guess. I always felt kind of invisible and detached. I think I believed that it was a way to be 'seen,' in a way, and when my boobs grew, I knew that I was qualified, in a way that I wasn't qualified for much else."

"But…"

"If I was taller and thinner, I would have tried to be a fashion model. If I had been any good at acting, I would have given that a go. I just wanted to be …visible…to myself too."

"You don't think it's…risky, being viewed as just a pair of boobs?"

"The money is great." The way she said it, automatically, as if she didn't mean it, got to Ceci, pained her. Emma's eyes were starting to close. Ceci, who was lying next to her on the bed, facing her, watched her long eyelashes descend like curtains.

A Place Called Home

The girls were dropped off at the same carpark in South London from which they had left. The midday sun glinting off all the parked cars made it look halfway pleasant, the bright sky reflected in the windows.

"Next tour in about a month, more or less, end of September, I believe." Ben unlocked the van and nodded to them as he dismissed them, like a cold-hearted and indifferent headmaster. "We'll be in touch."

"He makes everything sound ominous." Muttered Emma.

"We're home now, you can chill!" Becky sighed.

Ben had been quiet on the long drive, with the usual multiple stops at the service stations, but the atmosphere had been calm. The sun was shining fiercely and the heat in the van had made everyone even more drowsy than they were already. At least they had been allowed to wear their own clothes.

The girls still felt a bit weird, they still thought they might be suffering from some bug. Since the cocktail night, they had struggled to feel fully awake. Despite lengthy naps, work on that final night had been a struggle; it had felt like wading through honey. They hadn't given out nearly as many t-shirts as usual.

"I dumped a load of them on a chair outside the toilets in that last venue." Ceci had admitted to Nicole.

"Gosh, aren't you the rebel!" Nicole laughed. "I've been dumping those t-shirts in strategic places since the start!"

"Really?" Ceci was wide-eyed and a bit shocked, but glad, as ever, to have Nicole in her corner.

"Well, yeah, Ben should have come into the venues with us, like he was supposed to!" She shrugged and yawned simultaneously.

As the girls left the car park, stretching and lugging their bags, they promised to call each other and stay in touch.

Ceci and Nicole had made a more immediate, concrete plan. The idea was that Ceci would return to the bedsit and get as many of her things together as she could before going to Nicole's. The hope was that Stuart would be at work. Nicole would take Ceci's small suitcase home with her from the car park.

"Are you sure you can carry both bags?" Ceci frowned, "It's hot!"

"I'm big and tough, remember!" Nicole laughed and rolled her eyes, "It's a few stops on the train, don't worry."

Emma was relieved to be back home and especially away from Ben, even though the flat she shared looked like a complete hovel compared to the luxurious hotels they had been staying in for the last two weeks.

Funny how quickly they had all acclimatised to better things.

Letting herself in with her key, Emma wandered around the damp-smelling space, taking stock. The boys were clearly out, their presence was always loud and obvious in almost a performative way.

The two boy actors shared the twin-bedded larger room, and Emma had the single. It was so tiny, that it could easily have been described as a walk-in wardrobe, only it was attached to the kitchen and separated only by one of those bead curtains.

There was only space enough for a single bed and a thin rickety chest of drawers. Emma always tried to keep her things neatly piled up and stacked under the bed; that was the only way possible to contain her possessions in such a miniscule area. However, inevitably loose discarded photographs of her would gather dust, forgotten on the chest of drawers and when she was in London, her portfolio would live there too, at arms' reach. Her seascapes, oil on canvas, loomed down over the bed obscuring the cracks in the walls.

She thought then that she would start painting the river as soon as she could; her fingers itched to hold a brush.

The bathroom was attached to the boys' bedroom. The unorthodox layout of the flat alone meant that none of the three ever invited romantic partners back.

The tenants only stayed because it was extremely cheap, and probably it was only extremely cheap because no other sensible people would rent it. Observing it then, with the critical eyes of someone who had just seen better things, Emma was shocked: The wallpaper peeling and flaking off in large segments everywhere, cracks in the plaster on every conceivable surface, the vinyl floor of the kitchen bumpy and uneven as if the individual tiles were somehow shrivelling, the tiny beetles who had always resided in the kitchen cabinets rent free, regardless of how many times Emma tried to clean.

Emma was just heading towards the bathroom to continue her grim inventory, when Adam, one of the boys, came bustling in.

"Helloooo!" He cried in his best camp voice, coming towards Emma with his skinny arms wide and enveloping her in a bony hug. He was smothered in aftershave which was a welcome respite from the stench of damp which permeated the flat.

"How was it? Did you miss us?"

Emma smiled warmly, "Yes, actually, I really did!" And she realised that was true in spite of the revolting nature of the flat, she felt safe there.

"Have you seen the posters?"

"What posters?"

"That weird brand you're working for, they've put posters all over London! You must have seen them."

"How do you know it's the same brand?"

"Well…duh…it's just a white background with a purple question mark on it."

"Oh! Where are they?"

"Literally everywhere, the underground, billboards, on buses… you'll notice them in about five minutes next time you leave the flat."

"Have you had any thoughts about what the brand might be?" Emma knew her flatmates loved a mystery, a conspiracy theory even more so.

"They still haven't told you?" Adam was aghast. "All those weeks with them and you didn't work it out!"

Emma shook her head, laughing dryly.

"It wasn't like that, I just hung out with the other girls and honestly, we didn't really talk about it, we'd just discuss the money really."

For some reason, Emma didn't want to bring Ben into the conversation, she didn't even want to think about him.

"Ah, on the subject of money…"

The Money

The girls were paid even more than they thought they would be. The money went straight into their bank accounts on the day they returned from the tour and a payslip was mailed to their home address.

Sitting at the kitchen table in her parents' tidy home, the birds twittering at the bird feeder in the landscaped back garden, Becky stared wide-eyed at the payslip. Weirdly, her first gut reaction was shame, although, of course she had done nothing to be ashamed of. Maybe it was because she saw, had always seen, how hard her parents worked as doctors, a worthy profession, and there she was, getting a huge sum of money for nothing, well, for nonsense really.

Common sense kicked in then. Of course, she would use the money for something that would help her in her chosen career; acting courses say, or even singing. Agents were always insisting you needed to be able to sing and dance as well as act.

Becky folded the document up neatly and put it into the pocket of her dressing gown. She didn't want her parents to see it.

Meanwhile, on a different planet:

Nobody was awake in the flat that Sammy shared with her mother (and a miserable revolving door of her mother's unsuitable boyfriends,) when the letter from the bank slipped through the letterbox, as weightless and insubstantial as a threatening glance.

The night before, the evening of the day of the return, Sammy had gone to the pub with one of her long-standing friends from the estate. She had returned to the flat earlier with her pink suitcase and been mightily relieved to find her mother alone. Nevertheless, Sammy had no intention of spending the evening with her mother, watching her loll on the dirty sofa in her filthy dressing gown and get inebriated on cheap vodka. To that end, she had called her long-standing friend Tracey, and the two had headed to the local pub.

It was a relief, for Sammy, to be with someone who didn't seem to judge her or look down on her, and she would have liked to make a night of it. However, she, like the others, still felt weirdly fragile and excessively sleepy. Much to Tracey's disappointment, she had insisted on going home to sleep after a couple of drinks.

"Used to better things than this?" Tracey had swept her chubby arm, the bracelets tinkling against each other, around the dowdy pub, thick with the stench of cigarettes and decades of spilt beer. Sammy stood, swaying lightly, and shoving her cigarettes back in her bag, getting ready to go.

"Oh no," She shook her head and snorted, "It's not like that. Yeah, the hotels were fancy, but I didn't get on that well with the other girls, they were kind of snobby, to be honest. I'm glad to be back, well, not with my mum obviously, but back in London, back with you! You know what I mean."

"What happened with that driver bloke, the one you fancied?"

They were walking back through the estate in the pale summer gloaming, the sky an incongruously beautiful shade of cobalt blue. They could hear rustling in the undergrowth, voices behind brick walls and muttering in maze-like alleyways, firecrackers, the sound of motorbikes revving. It was not animals that worried them. Both girls knew the dangers of the estate all too well and tried to stick to the illuminations provided by the sporadic orange lamp posts.

"Oh, nothing happened with him." Sammy blushed and kept her face hidden from her friend's curious gaze. "He was a bit weird, more than that actually, a bit of a dick."

Tracey nodded sagely in the half-light. Both girls, but Sammy in particular, had had more than their share of unfortunate experiences with men, often those who had seemed initially promising. (Or had they? Had she just been clutching at straws?)

The next morning, when Sammy finally woke and noticed the envelope on the grubby doormat, it was Tracey whom she called.

Tracey had a small child, a toddler, and lived still with her mother, but it was a far happier set up than Sammy's own.

The toddler always screeched when Tracey was on the phone though, and it was screeching then. Normally, the sound irritated Sammy, but she had her payslip in one hand and for one second, she was blissfully happy.

"You can move out now! That's it, you'll be free of her!" Tracey shouted over her child.

"Not quite yet. A few more of these tours and then I'll definitely be out of here, for good!"

Ceci's reaction when she saw the envelope with the payslip in Nicole's hand the following day, was panic.

The plan that the two of them had concocted for the preceding day had gone like clockwork. Stuart had been out, fortuitously, when Ceci had returned to remove her stuff from the bedsit.

In a sweaty, flustered hurry, she had shoved everything that was hers into bin bags (she didn't own another case and she had no intention of taking anything from Stuart) and lugged her ungainly haul across London and to Nicole's flat.

Nicole had opened the door to Ceci and laughed.

"Someone needs a shower urgently!" Ceci was indeed bright red of face and dripping with sweat, her hands clutching at the bags with a claw-like grip.

That evening, they had celebrated Ceci's freedom with Chantal, who accepted her presence amicably and unquestioningly. They ordered a takeaway and opened a bottle of wine.

Ceci had felt as if a weight was lifted, but now, looking at the envelope in Nicole's hand, she felt a sickening.

"Too much smugness yesterday, my own stupid fault."

"What are you talking about?" Nicole was happily distracted.

"The letter with the payslip will arrive at the bedsit. He'll see it and open it!"

"And so? It's your money! He can't get to it!"

"Yeah, but he knows I have it now! He probably would have let me go, but now, he could chase me for this money, for part of it at least, on the grounds that I owe him for the rent or whatever! He'll use it as an excuse, don't you see?"

"Pfft!" Nicole was far too excited to start discussing Stuart again. "You're worrying too much!"

About the Money

Emma had always intended to help her flatmates with the rent, they didn't need to persuade her, but, at the same time, she vaguely resented the fact that her (substantial) new wages were kind of expected, almost, to go into the common kitty.

"After your next tour thing, we'll have enough to move out and find a better flat!" Enthused Adam.

"We? Maybe in the meantime, you will get a paid acting gig and then you can be the big breadwinner!"

The sarcasm went over Adam's head.

"Yeah," He sighed deeply and lit a cigarette, holding it gracefully in his elegant hand. "That's unlikely to happen." His tone was mournful, yet also somehow resigned, and Emma realised that she was somehow stuck providing for this, her new, makeshift family.

She wasn't sure how she felt about that. She searched under her bed for her large sketching pad, and brought it to the kitchen table. She always made preliminary sketches before painting, it was part of her ritual.

"More seascapes?"

"No, a river this time." Emma replied, relieved to be able to work on her art, but also troubled, a not insignificant portion of her mind haunted by the stinking dark swirling water.

Emma didn't call her agency. She didn't feel like going to castings and especially not like taking her top off.

She just wanted to paint.

Grief came often for Sammy in the night. It had haunted her for years. It woke her and she would lie in it until her heart stopped pounding and she would try to think of happy places, of times she had been at peace. Those unreliable, transient wisps of memory, jostled unsuccessfully against all the toxic memories, which seemed to be far more powerful and all-consuming.

"Money." She thought then, immediately as she woke and she grinned into the darkness. The cheap digital clock on her bedside table informed her that it was just after three, and noises were coming from her mother's bedroom. The grin left her face immediately. Instinctively, she peered through the gloom at her bedroom door to check that the lock was in place.

Sammy wasn't taking any chances.

In theory, the girls could have been hunting for other work until the next tour, but with the date rapidly approaching and with all that money already in the bank, the urgency simply wasn't there.

Nicole and Ceci shared a room and the atmosphere was so convivial that Ceci cursed herself for putting up with Stuart for so long. Nicole did go out for a few modelling castings and did a few shows, and Ceci was more than happy to stay with Chantal and keep her company. Chantal was good humoured and easy going and enjoyed the company of young people. She founded Brenda too sanctimonious often, and it was a relief for her to spend time with 'the youth' as she always referred to Nicole's friends.

It had always troubled Chantal that Nicole had very few friends, barely any.

"I should really be looking for my own place." Ceci repeated, almost on a daily basis.

"What for?" Nicole would roll her eyes every time she made that suggestion. "We're getting on well, aren't we? Plenty of time after the next tour and the next chunk of money."

It wasn't just the surprisingly strong bond that they had forged that kept Ceci in Nicole's flat, however. There was something reassuring about residing in a place with multiple locks on the door. Ceci didn't discuss it, not even with Nicole, but she was reluctant to go out. It was irrational, she knew, especially given the size of London, but she was worried about suddenly bumping into Stuart. On several occasions, she would get dressed to leave and then stand in front of the heavy door and find herself frozen in place. She did, just about, manage to accompany Nicole to the local supermarket, but even that was ludicrously stressful. Her heart rate would accelerate whenever she saw any man of the same size as Stuart, and she was constantly on high alert.

"You need to chill!" Nicole would sigh, on repeat, "You just know Stuart is not hiding behind the tins in this tiny supermarket on this crappy estate waiting for you!"

"I know that, I do!" Ceci would agree, miserably.

"And even if he did suddenly appear, I would punch him and that would be that!" Nicole would always say things like that to cheer Ceci up, and Ceci would pretend it worked.

Ceci and Chantal often chatted about other possibilities for Ceci. One of the options that Ceci somehow kept returning to was pursuing a university education. Chantal, albeit possibly humouring her, seemed enthusiastic about the idea and to that end they sent off for various university prospectuses to arrive at the flat.

Nicole found it vaguely amusing, when she returned from her castings or her job, to find her mother and Ceci sitting together and pouring over a glossy prospectus in the shabby living room, discussing the merits of various courses.

As if it was that easy. Still, she did nothing to burst Ceci's bubble. Life was hard enough.

Becky, meanwhile, as industrious as ever, work ethic if not academic brains inherited from her parents, did immediately contact her agents again to tell them that she was available until the next tour.

"Hmm," the agent grumbled, "You'll be kind of hampered time wise until these tours are finished with, for anything beyond commercials certainly."

"I'm very happy with commercials!" Becky grinned, knowing she would be lucky to get them.

She also enrolled into a twice weekly dance class especially for musical theatre which she thought might prove useful.

Sammy's agent at her promotion's agency, when Sammy called her, was much friendlier than she had ever been.

"Not sure we can find you anything of the calibre you're now used to, Sammy!" She trilled, clearly delighted with herself.

For a few brief seconds, Sammy smiled too and then, suddenly, she stopped.

A realisation came to her with great, with astounding, clarity.

Second Tour: Setting off

Leaves were trodden on, wet and slimy, in the car park as the girls and their managers reconvened to set off on the second tour. The first hints of Autumn were in the air, there was a bitter bite to the breeze although the sun still glared defiantly down on them all.

The girls had been spotting ads for their mysterious brand all over London since they had returned from the first tour, and there, in that very car park was a huge billboard just above the area where the vans were waiting, just the white background with the huge purple painted question mark.

The girls had almost moved beyond caring what the product was by then, all they were interested in was the money. Having seen it in their bank accounts once, where before there had been nothing, they were all greedy for more.

There was no fanfare this time, no speeches, the girls all just arrived and walked straight over to their team and their van. A couple of the purple question mark stickers had peeled off.

They all hugged each other and mumbled a shy hello to Ben. He seemed in a friendly mood, to be fair, although he had undergone a severe haircut, a buzzcut, which rendered his appearance even more bullish and threatening.

The girls were all in uniform for that first drive and surreptitiously, they all glanced at each other. Sammy seemed to have lost some weight; the waistband of her jeans was no longer digging into her stomach. Her face was lightly tanned though, in a natural way, and she was wearing far less make-up than before. She looked much better for it.

Emma, too, seemed tinier than they all remembered, as if she had shrunk, but unlike Sammy, she looked gaunt and pale, weirdly so considering the summer they had had.

"You'd look like that too if I hadn't made you sit outside!" Nicole muttered to Ceci, and Ceci acknowledged that was true. Nicole had made her sit with Chantal out on the walkway in front of their flat to catch the sun.

"It will do you both good. Can't have the pair of you withering away like a couple of Victorian ladies!" She had instructed, and she had been right.

Strangely, Ceci's stomach seemed to have calmed down too since she had been staying with Nicole. Maybe the bloating really was all stress related.

Becky was glowing, on the other hand, and immediately started regaling the others with anecdotes from her dancing course, where, apparently, she had met loads of new people, and had an excellent time socialising with them.

"What did you do?" She asked Emma as they squashed into the van, next to each other.

"I painted." Said Emma curtly and then stared out of the window deliberately as if she didn't want to speak.

Nicole raised her eyebrows at Becky silently and Becky shrugged. Nicole would have imagined that those two would have stayed in touch during the break but apparently not.

"Let's be off then!" Announced Ben, with uncommon cheer, as he manoeuvred the van out of the car park and rock music blared from the speakers.

"Here we go again!" Muttered Ceci, rolling her eyes, taking care first that Ben couldn't see her face in the mirror.

Ceci had felt strange leaving the cocoon of Nicole and Chantal's flat and taking the train to get back on the van. She knew it was illogical, all of it, not least that she had apparently settled down in someone else's home and, to all intents and purposes now lived there (she had left all her stuff there). Nicole and Chantal, to their credit could not have been more welcoming. Nicole insisted, in fact, that Ceci was doing her a huge favour by staying with Chantal. If it hadn't been for Ceci, they would have had to tolerate a lot more of Brenda, or pay for a carer, which had been the original plan.

Nevertheless, the situation was unsustainable. Ceci knew that she could not stay there forever, and to that end, she was determined to move out once they had returned from this tour.

It was morning when they left London and three hours later, they had not yet reached their destination. Anticipation and excitement at seeing each other had dwindled away and they all dozed and stared out of the windows, tired of trying to chat over the ubiquitous rock music.

Subconsciously, they had all waited to see if Ben would pull in at every service station as before, and he had done, exactly as before.

Still an addict, thought Nicole grimly, but obviously did not say anything.

It was four o'clock by the time they arrived at their hotel. It was recognisably from the same chain they had stayed in before, and there was something slightly comforting about that, although the novelty value of staying in a fancy hotel had all but dissipated.

Tough Town

As they pulled into the car park of the hotel, Ben turned off his music and spoke to the girls. He had barely said anything on the lengthy trip up the motorway and the sound of his deep voice jolted them wide awake.

"This town, actually all of them on this tour are a bit rougher than the ones we went to last time. I just need you to be aware that there is lots of poverty and deprivation around these parts. It doesn't always bring out the best in people as I'm sure you're aware."

The girls nodded. The hotel, as they lugged their cases up to reception, looked exactly the same as it always did, same furnishings, same colour scheme. Of course it did, it was part of the same chain.

The manager, a pale man with a strange tuft of white blond hair, appeared to be very well acquainted with Ben. The two slapped each other on the back and shook hands. Out of the corner of his eye, the man ran his eyes over the girls as if he was assessing livestock. He muttered something to Ben, who laughed.

Nicole saw this as did Sammy. The two exchanged a weary glance. Both were relieved Emma had not witnessed it, she was already being weird. Her break had not, apparently, helped her relax.

In the rooms, same allocation as before, Sammy immediately put her bag down on the fold out bed without the need for argument. Ceci was relieved. She was tense after Ben's speech about how rough the town was. She had spent so long indoors, she was worried about her capability of doing the job in any location, she was no longer used to speaking to people, to being out and about. Her existence, during the last month, had shrunk to the size of a rundown flat. She was also concerned her stomach would start cramping again. Even worrying about it could bring it on. A no-win situation.

There was not much time before they had to get ready for work. The girls ordered room service and slumped on their beds watching a film. The hotel was situated in a type of industrial estate, offices, and warehouses all around. In front was the usual car park and their rooms at the back overlooked a huge metal oblong building which could have been used for anything, it wasn't clear.

"Not the best view…" Sighed Emma staring outside as the sun set, glinting and reflecting against the metal.

"Oh, it's fine, at least it's not raining!" Replied Becky, perky as usual.

"Hmm. I've been painting rivers, you know, at home."

"Oh, yes?" Inwardly Becky sighed. Not this again, she thought.

"I've tried to diversify, to paint something else, but it just doesn't…I don't know, it just doesn't come to me. Whenever I try to think of anything else, the only thing I can imagine is a river."

"I think you need to get out more, be around people more, no wonder you get all wrapped up in your own thoughts when you barely see anyone else!" Becky struggled to keep the exasperation out of her voice.

"I see my flatmates." Said Emma in a small defensive voice.

"I mean other people. Also, your flatmates go out, I know they do! I see them! Why don't you go out with them at least?"

"Yeah, I don't know…it's just, I don't feel like it."

"What about your family, when was the last time you saw them?"

"Before the summer, and they very rarely come up to London, I tend to go down to them."

"Maybe you should…"

"What?"

"Go and see them! After this tour?"

"I…I don't know, I'll see.

" Emma turned away from Becky as if to signify the end of discussion.

Becky sighed again, inwardly. She didn't want the responsibility of looking after Emma, she didn't feel qualified.

They were all varying degrees of nervous when they met later at the van. Nicole was thinking that Ben probably shouldn't have mentioned that this town was tough, now they were all on edge. It was colder there then in London too. They shivered in their t-shirts as they gathered on the tarmac.

In the event however, despite their initial nerves, that evening was completely bearable, much better than they expected. The pubs were pleasantly warm and stuffy with the cigarette fumes and omnipresent stench of beer. Maybe the clientele in the pubs were a bit rougher around the edges, it was hard to tell. In any case, they were polite enough to the girls and two of the later pubs, when people tended to get sloppy drunk and irritating, were student pubs, so that was fine. The girls felt like they knew where they were with the students.

On the way back to the hotel in the van, they relaxed, (even Emma laughed at some corny joke,) so relieved they were that the evening had gone well. It had felt, at the start, like a hurdle to get over, especially after Ben's warning.

When Ben suggested a drink at the hotel bar as they pulled into the car park, there seemed no polite reason to refuse.

Ben's Friend

None of the girls went up to their room to get changed, not even Sammy. The others wondered about that. Sammy seemed different in general, but one of the most significant differences was that she seemed to be entirely uninterested, suddenly, in flirting with Ben.

Ben led the way to a table in the bar of the hotel. The blonde hotel manager was already sitting there with a beer in front of him. Aha. Unease settled over all of them like a fever. Clearly this had been pre-arranged.

The shock of white blonde hair contrasted badly with his pale blotchy skin. As the girls approached, a smirk played about his face.

"Hi! Hi! I am Peter, how lovely to make the acquaintance of you lovely ladies! Drinks are on me!"

Emma literally froze in her tracks when she saw him sitting there.

"What the fuck is this?" She muttered.

Becky, right behind her, prodded her in the back.

"Doesn't matter what it is in their tiny brains, we'll have one drink and go to bed!" She whispered firmly.

"Does seem like some kind of sleazy ambush, for sure." whispered Ceci.

"Sleazy is right!" Nicole remembered the enthusiastic greeting between the two men earlier. Had it been planned then or before?

The girls asked for wine and watched, with subconscious care, as the girl behind the bar poured it into their glasses and lined them up. Peter made to fetch them, but Nicole and Ceci jumped up quickly instead. Becky ordered juice.

It was Nicole who was sitting next to Peter. On his other side was Ben, looking smug. His side of the bargain had been fulfilled apparently. To herself, Nicole mused, that she was probably not Peter's first choice. Yet she saw it as her responsibility, somehow, to protect the other, more vulnerable girls.

"How do you two know each other?" She asked, widening her eyes deliberately in feigned innocence.

"Oh, we go way back, way back…" Peter's gaze was evasive as he gripped his beer, his eyes of a weak, watery blue. Like diluted paint thought Emma, who was staring at him fixedly. Blue paint mixed with dirty rainwater.

"And now you both find yourselves in this hotel, in this town, what a great coincidence!" Commented Nicole with faux enthusiasm.

Ben gave her a sharp look.

"It's a small world sometimes. Drink up! There's more where that came from."

He turned to Sammy, clearly just as bemused as the rest of them as to why she wasn't being as chatty and flirty as usual.

"What's up with you Sammy? You seem a bit…deflated."

Sammy grinned but it was obviously forced.

"I don't know, just feeling a bit tired suddenly."

"This job is not for tired people girls! Remember what they told you at the casting; enthusiasm, adaptability and friendliness are called for!"

Ben's tone seemed neutral but there was a glint in his dark eyes, a tension in his meaty jaws that seemed to signify a determination that they perform, that they adhere to…what?

Some creed of unstoppable friendliness? Did they have to be friendly to the creepy manager too? Was he telling them that was what they had signed up to?

A pact with the devil, thought Emma, breathing deeply and audibly. Becky kicked her under the table.

"Sorry." Muttered Sammy confused. She seemed to think that his comment was aimed at her and her alone.

"I wasn't just talking to you, Sammy, I meant all of you. I'm going to the bathroom now, by the time I return, with more drinks, I expect all of you to be at your best!"

Ben got up and stormed off. The girls glanced at each other nervously. Peter laughed uproariously with his mouth wide open. His back teeth were yellow and filled with broken silver filaments.

"I guess he told you off good and proper!" He sneered.

"Remember who pays your wages that's what I always say!"

"Do you, Peter? Is that what you always say?" Nicole opened her eyes wide again, made her voice fake and silky. Inside fury was rising like an unstoppable torrent.

Ceci kicked her under the table. Emma looked like she was about to faint. Becky was, as usual, the most unfazed.

They could see Ben had stopped at the bar, when Peter got up abruptly and stumbled in the direction of the toilet.

"Look!" Nicole turned to the others and hissed with urgency.

"This is shit, this little powerplay but we have to pretend to play along whilst we can, as long as it doesn't get too awful so that we get our next cash instalment, I know we all need it, I know it makes a difference to all of us!"

"I'm not flirting with that Peter creep!"

"Do you think they'll get rid of us? Really?"

"If we're too 'hostile', yes, yes, they will, we are totally replaceable!"

"It's not worth the money." That was Emma. "None of this shit is worth the money." Her tone was almost forlorn.

"They're coming back now, let's just try and make it until the end of the tour!"

Adaptability

That evening they did make an immense effort to be polite at least. All of them except Emma who was incapable apparently and had to be repeatedly kicked by Becky. They sipped politely at their second drinks, but did not get drunk even slightly, let alone sloppy drunk or particularly congenial.

They may have pretended to relax, but they did not. Their muscles were tense and they were completely alert.

Clearly Ben had expected a different outcome for Peter or even for himself and he was disappointed and obviously annoyed and yet he couldn't exactly spell it out. He dismissed them after the second drink and prolonged artificial efforts at desultory conversation.

"Get a good night's sleep…I hope you feel more energetic tomorrow." You'd better do, was unsaid.

"Are we going to have to hang out with that creep every night?" Asked Ceci when they were back in the room.

"Maybe." Nicole replied gloomily. "While we're in this town at least."

"I've met worse." muttered Sammy who was sitting on the fold out bed and brushing her hair.

"What *is* up with you, by the way? You don't seem yourself?"

"You barely know me!" Scoffed Sammy.

"Yeah, you're right, sorry." acknowledged Nicole cautiously, "But you did *seem* much more, um, extrovert on the last tour…"

"I guess…" Sammy stopped brushing but knelt with the brush in her lap. "I guess I finally realised how people saw me, the way my old promo agency saw me, as trash, and I, well, I started thinking about that…"

"I'm sure that's not true!"

"Don't even start! I know what you lot all think of me, especially you, Nicole, Miss fashion model, you're the worst! To you I'm just some trashy blonde, flirty and tarty."

Nicole swallowed nervously. "I…"

"You think I wouldn't like to be a 'real' model like you? Some of us don't have that body and don't get that choice, us poor, uneducated, non-beautiful people, our choices are severely fucking curtailed right from the start!"

Painful as it was to acknowledge the truth of that, Nicole and Ceci both realised it was so.

"I'm not a real model either!" interjected Ceci.

"No, but you are not considered 'trashy' or 'tacky' like me, you're just an ordinary girl."

"Yay!" Ceci tried to interject a lighter note.

It didn't work. Nicole felt guilty.

"Look, as things stand, we are all in the same boat here. We all of us need the money and we need to stick together. So far, we haven't had to put up with much in terms of creepy men, but we don't know what's ahead. In my view, there is something suspicious about the money they are paying us, it's way more than the going rate for any promotion, we all know it…"

"Yes, but it could just be a really wealthy company paying for it, couldn't it?"

"Yes, yes it could, and I am really hoping it's just that…"

"But," protested Ceci, "What I really don't get is why, if they want hookers, they don't just get hookers?"

"Because there is no thrill in that, no conquest."

Sammy turned the floor lamp off, the light that was near her bed and the other girls turned their bedside lamps off too. All three of them lay in the darkness wide-eyed, listening to the sound of distant traffic, the aroma of the alien sheets on their skin.

The following few days were calm. The girls got back into their routine from the previous tour. Despite Ben's warnings that the town was rough, it honestly didn't seem it. Not during the day when they wandered about it, and not at night in the pubs. Certainly no rougher than the towns on the previous tour.

A cold spell had settled over that part of the UK, and Autumn was in full swing. The girls wore jumpers and jackets and walked through the pretty green spaces of the town watching the students congregating and feeling, as before, no small twinge of envy. In that place too, the question mark ads were everywhere and sometimes young people who frequented the pubs at night, often students, approached the girls when they saw them in town.

Mainly, they tried to coax more info about the product from the girls. Unsuccessfully, of course.

Sometimes the girls made a game of spotting people wearing a question mark t-shirt. That had been more successful during the previous tour when the weather was warmer.

The Neverending Peter

On the last night in that town, in the way back in the van, Ben told them they were going for a drink.

"Best behaviour please." He said gruffly as he opened the doors to the van to let them out.

"I knew we were going to have to tolerate that Peter again!"

"Why can't we just say no?"

"You know why! We've been through this! They're dangling the next cheque over our heads."

"What about if we complain about Ben?"

"Are you kidding? He is literally our manager! Who do you think has more power? Who do you think they'd listen to?"

"Who would we even complain to? Our agencies? Are you kidding?"

Glumly, they walked into the hotel and into the bar. Peter was sitting at the same table as before. In front of him were five cocktails.

In the doorway still, Emma clutched Ceci's arm, she was the closest.

"I'm not doing this," She said, her voice wavering but determined. "I just can't, I'm sorry."

With that she turned on her heel and ran up the stairs towards their rooms.

"Oh!" exclaimed Peter, his voice thick with faux concern, "Where is the little one going?"

"She…ate something dodgy at lunchtime, I think…"

"A burger!"

"Yes, that was it. She feels sick."

Peter knew they were lying of course, the same repulsive smirk sat upon his face, his eyes cold, empty somehow. Nicole somehow sitting closest to him again, shuddered.

"I don't drink, I'm afraid," Becky eyed the cocktail, "I'm Muslim."

"Of course you do!" Declared Peter, "No one really follows those crappy rules, do they? I've met plenty of Muslims who drink!"

"I do," Becky's voice was quiet but determined, and Nicole was filled with admiration. "I do follow the rules."

Ben was there again then, after his obligatory visit to the bathroom.

"This one won't drink." Peter complained to Ben, his voice a whine.

Ben sighed. "Yeah, it's fine." He didn't sound as if it was fine, merely as if he couldn't be bothered to argue about it. "I'll get her a juice."

The girls sat looking at their cocktails.

"They're not bombs, they're not going to explode! Drink up!" Peter clearly thought he was hilarious.

All the girls were pushing against each other under the table in any way that they could; knees, elbows feet. All they had was each other, that was how they felt.

"Remind me of your room allocation?" Ben asked, "Who's sharing with who again?"

"Why?" asked Nicole.

Ben looked affronted, more than affronted. "I'm your manager, I have every right to know. Is it supposed to be a secret from me? Didn't I designate your rooms at the start?"

Ceci distracted herself by reminding herself of the extended period of time when she was worried about Stuart tracking her down. She hadn't thought about Stuart in days.

These two were more scary somehow, and crucially, right there.

Trapped, the girls sipped at their cocktails warily. They didn't taste extremely alcoholic, just very sweet. Becky had a juice. Becky would be a witness thought Nicole, she knew the juice was not doctored, she had seen it being poured and Becky had collected it. A second later, while Ben was regaling them with some elaborate boastful anecdote which they were only half listening to, Nicole wondered if she was being paranoid, whether Emma, who was clearly losing the plot, was somehow contagious.

Maybe these men, although obviously not particularly worthy individuals, didn't have nefarious intentions? Maybe they just wanted a drink with some pretty girls, maybe that was all it was?

The Hangover

The following morning, they were due to check out at eleven and drive to the next town. Becky had forced Emma out of bed and down to breakfast around nine. Fortunately, the appeal of helping themselves liberally from the breakfast buffet had not worn off, not even for Emma.

The hotel restaurant was empty except for the two girls, the buffet pristine and untouched. Usually, there was at least one member of staff on hand, but not then. It seemed eerie somehow; the silence broken only by the slow drip of the coffee pot, a distant vacuum cleaner, the omnipresent hum from some unseen industrial fridge.

The windows of the restaurant looked onto the hotel parking lot which was empty bar a few normal cars and then their van which gleamed mammoth and white and faintly sinister in the bright sunlight.

"Shame there's no river here." Said Emma.

"Hmm." Mumbled Becky. She could not tolerate any more nonsense about rivers from Emma, that was how she felt. In any case, she was preoccupied, worrying about the other three. It was very unusual for them to miss breakfast. Also, they had seemed excessively drunk the night before, considering they had each drunk only two cocktails.

"They don't even have paintings of rivers." Added Emma sadly, chewing on a croissant.

It was true. There were prints of pink flowers everywhere in that hotel. Carnations in vases, not very creative or original. In the restaurant there was, above the buffet, a huge print of a bouquet of multicoloured flowers.

"Not pink at least!" Becky smiled at Emma. It felt to her like humouring a sulky, unpredictable child.

After breakfast, the two of them went to bang on the door of the other three, the room just next to theirs. Despite repeated and ferocious banging, there was no reply. Becky, anxiety and unease starting to blossom within her, put her ear to the door. No sound could be heard from within, no movement.

Emma grabbed Becky's arm, her tiny nails digging in.

"Do you think they're OK? Do you think they might be dead?"

Her voice rose, breathless and hysterical.

"Calm down!" Becky had found that Emma responded better to commands issued in a firm voice. "Of course, they're not dead, don't be ridiculous! They are merely extremely hungover and most likely deeply asleep still."

Silently, Becky crossed her fingers and prayed it was so.

She persuaded Emma to return to their own room and they both packed in silence. Emma in the prison of fear she had already concocted in her head and Becky with a very rational anxiety starting to rage through her.

Becky almost cried with relief and Emma did actually cry when they heard banging and shouts on their own door not twenty minutes later. It was the unmistakeable sound of Nicole and Ceci, swearing and complaining.

"Why the hell didn't you wake us?" Nicole standing in the corridor half dressed, looked dreadful, as did Ceci. They appeared not only bedraggled and somehow unsteady on their feet, but their skin looked ashy and grey.

"You think we didn't try? What is wrong with you? You look absolutely terrible. If that's what alcohol does, I'm glad I don't get involved!"

"Alcohol doesn't usually do this, no…" Ceci, slumped against the wall of the corridor, tried to shake her head but winced and screwed her eyes shut.

"I feel like there is a literal drum being banged in my head. This is awful."

"Truth." Nicole was propping herself up by leaning on the door frame. "I cannot remember ever having a hangover like this before, it feels…"

"Feels a bit like when we thought we were ill after the cocktails on the first tour, but like a million times worse." That was Ceci. They were inside Becky and Emma's room by then, Nicole and Ceci slumped on the beds.

They all looked at each other. Nicole and Ceci seemed to have aged weirdly overnight. There were deep violet circles under their eyes.

"If he's drugging us, why? To what end?"

"I don't know but he asked for the room allocation again."

"Yes, but again, why? For what purpose?"

"Look, we can't deal with this now, we have to go, where's Sammy?"

"We couldn't wake her!"

"Well, you'll have to! Go!"

Protection

In the van for the transfer to the next town, a cold drizzle, a colourless sky. Even with make-up, the faces of the three who had struggled to wake were sickly blotched, deeply etched with under-eye bags.

"No more partying for you girls!" declared Ben, with a revolting smugness to his tone, and the girls pressed their knees and elbows against each other in the show of solidarity which was becoming somehow vital.

Rock music blared and nausea settled on Ceci, Nicole, and Sammy like a second skin as the car sped and swerved.

Nobody spoke.

It was only a couple of hours until the next place and yet Ben stopped at a service station as he always did. Usually Nicole would take mental note, but she was feeling too sick and like Ceci and Sammy, struggling frantically to recall what happened in between drinking the cocktails and waking up that morning feeling like death.

"I wonder why we all need the money." Emma's small voice piped up, almost conversational and yet with the increasing undertone of mania.

"Not now, Emma!" Hissed Nicole, "We all feel like shit, definitely not the time for a philosophical discussion."

In the same way that Ben did not like air conditioning in the car, neither did he like heating, but the unpleasantly frigid air was, at least, going some way to wake them up and keep them alert.

Only Becky was untroubled on that drive. She gazed out of the window at the sodden green and grey landscape and thought, happily, of all she could do with the next instalment of cash.

When they arrived at the hotel in the next town (seemingly smaller and rumoured to be quaint), Nicole, Ceci and Sammy retired immediately back to bed.

They never argued anymore about bed allocation, just automatically taking turns with the fold out bed.

"Someone shut the blinds and the curtains, I thought I was going to die in that van, I felt so rough." Sammy flopped down on the bed with her eyes closed. She was so pale that she looked green.

"We have proof that it's not a bug this time because the other two are absolutely fine."

"Yes, it was the cocktails and this is not a normal hangover, he or that creep, Peter, doctored them, but why?"

"He's not going to fucking tell us, is he?" Nicole sighed, despondent, but also furious. "Whatever this shit is, we can't let him win!"

"OK, we finish the tour and get the money unless something else happens, agreed?"

"Hmm…we have to be alert, you get me? No more cocktails and we watch him like a hawk!"

"Like hawks, don't you mean?"

The three of them slept all day whilst Becky made Emma go for a walk. It was bitterly cold, but at least the drizzle had abated, and they were snug in jumpers and jackets. Emma was delighted to discover that there was a river that meandered charmingly through the centre of the town, the banks festooned with late blooming flowers.

"Maybe you can introduce flowers when you paint your river pics!" Becky suggested brightly as Emma seemed in quite a congenial mood.

"Maybe." Emma nodded, distracted as usual. Increasingly, she seemed lost in her own world and disconnected from reality.

The girls followed the river as it flowed past the town and through the fields. By then, the path was more sparsely populated by dog walkers, stooped old men, laughing gaggles of scruffy students (because it seemed as if this town was a student town too).

Fields on either side of the river were dotted with cows and the girls stopped to lean over the fences and try to entice them near. In the next field there were sheep, their wool knotted and filthy, expressions blank.

"I thought I saw Peter." Emma stated then, staring at a sheep bleating close to them, her hair swishing messily against her face. The roots needed doing.

"What? No, Peter was in in the last town, you're getting muddled up."

"No, he was here, in this town, next to that pub in the centre."

Becky stared at Emma's profile, but she looked oddly serene. Her features were small, doll-like, and without the assistance of make-up, childlike and plain.

She decided that her best bet was to change the subject, so she did and Peter was not mentioned again.

By the time they met in the carpark at 7.30, the poorly girls felt marginally better, but certainly not normal.

They worked the first pub on autopilot, their voices robotic, the script second nature by then. They barely looked at the people to whom they were handing out the t-shirts.

It was at the second pub that there was a disturbance.

Nicole felt a man push against her and she realised, with a kind of delayed astonishment, that someone was trying to grab the bag full of t-shirts from her shoulder.

Nicole's initial reaction was total bemusement because it was such an unnecessary theft. She had every intention of handing out the shirts to anyone who wanted one. She frequently gave out more than she was supposed too anyway. By then, they all did.

She resisted. She was afraid of repercussions if she lost the bag. The man, more of a boy, her age, skinny, gathered his mates and suddenly she found herself surrounded. None of them were particularly large or threatening. Nicole was accustomed to far more sinister characters on her estate, and yet it was the sheer quantity of them that was intimidating.

Having successfully jostled the cloth bag of t-shirts off her shoulder, they formed a circle around her and started lobbing it to each other, exactly like a playground bully would with a school bag. Nicole was becoming increasingly worried off course, but at the same time, a tiny part of her was laughing at how farcical it was.

Clearly these boys did not know what she was capable of.

Barely had she had that thought when Ben appeared. That was shocking, in itself, as he had never gone into the pubs with them, not once. Ben grabbed the bag, in one fell swoop, and the boys did a runner, clearly deciding that he was too big to mess with, or maybe worrying that there was more than one of him.

Night

"Good thing that I was there to protect you." Ben declared in the van on the way to the next pub. The girls, having seen or heard what happened had huddled round Nicole, touching her and asking her if she was OK. Now, in the van, Ceci still had her hand placed gently on Nicole's arm in a gesture of silent solidarity.

"How did you know there was trouble?" Nicole asked over the throbbing base of the music. No reply came. Nicole thought they may not have heard her so she repeated the question.

She was waiting to hear that one of the other girls had gone out and alerted him, but no one said anything, and into the silence, his voice booming above the music, sounded somehow forced.

"I was going in to use the gents and I saw them hassling you, that's my job, innit, protection?"

Nicole and the other girls stared out into the darkness punctuated by blurred yellow street lights. It was cold in the van, but she felt a strange heat glow within her.

The rest of that night was calm.

On the final night in that town, they waited with dread to hear Ben mention a drink in the hotel bar, but he did not and relief propelled them, together, to hang out all in the one bigger room.

"Perhaps we should all sleep together, share beds in one room for protection?"

It was Emma who had spoken. She had seemed almost normal the last few days, quiet, but almost normal. The day before Ben had told her that she needed to dye her roots which were showing and she had calmly responded that she would.

Then, when she spoke about protection, they all stared at her.

"I'm interested, Emma," Nicole spoke gently, "What is it that you think we need protection from?" Deep down, she was beginning to wonder whether Emma had a point.

"From whatever it is that they are planning." Her voice was oddly matter of fact, and it was that which was somehow the most chilling.

"What do you think it is?"

"I have no idea, but it's not good and it likely involves sex."

Becky tried to laugh it off, as she always did with Emma's weirdness. "Gosh, not this again, Emma please! It's a very organised promotion job for a wealthy corporate company, there is absolutely nothing sinister or sexy, even, about it. Look at how we're dressed, jeans and t-shirts for one! It's hardly provocative!"

"All the same." Said Emma in a tone that sounded exactly like 'you will see.'

Emma was a bit nuts though, wasn't she? They all knew that. They all wanted to dismiss what she said as the paranoid ramblings of a mad girl, and yet, only Becky somehow fully succeeded. The others felt unease settle on them like a second skin.

Silence fell over the town. Somewhere there was a spike of female laughter along a nearby corridor. Further away, there was the deep monotonous hum of the motorway. The girls lay sprawled on the beds with a movie playing on the TV, subtitles on, sound low.

Ceci drifted off to a deep sleep next to Emma who lay awake on her back, her eyes wide. Nicole and Becky half-dosed and Sammy smoked out of the window into the shadowy darkness of the car park. Out of all of them, Sammy was the only one who smoked constantly and in the hotel rooms as well.

"I'm addicted," She would shrug, "If I didn't smoke, I would be the size of a house."

She threw the butt of her cigarette out and peered at Emma who was watching her with wide eyes, like some small wary mammal.

"What is wrong with you, Emma? When we all met, you seemed…normal, well as normal as anyone is, and a glamour model! I mean, it implies a certain confidence?"

"I don't know, it hit me suddenly, I guess, how vulnerable we are, and then…"

"Who? Who is vulnerable?"

"Well…us girls, all of us, doing these jobs that depend on our looks, on our 'friendliness' as they keep telling us, our 'adaptability', we need the money, most of us, well, basically all of us have little else and so we depend on some brutish man, Ben in this case…and…" Tears started spilling from her eyes and down her cheeks, her voice became breathless, "and…I felt suddenly…more than anything, I could see it all so clearly, I can see it all too clearly, it is …lonely…"

"OK, but…I understand your family don't know what you do?"

"It's not just that. I have always felt lonely with them too, kind of detached, as if there was a thick wall of glass between me and them. I don't know how else to describe it."

Sammy swallowed. She understood loneliness very well.

"What about friends?"

Emma snorted. "I don't really have friends, and I've realised that my flatmates, who I kind of thought of as my friends, are now far more interested in the money this is bringing in than in me. I feel, I feel…I don't know, more than anything, I feel like we're on the precipice of something, something bad…"

Bond

The last town of that tour was ugly and industrial and the citizens had barely any teeth. They were grateful for their t-shirts and the girls, in pity, gave them more than one, sometimes shoving two or three at them in a somewhat pointless gesture of generosity.

At night, without discussing it, the girls had somehow cemented the habit of sleeping all together in the bigger room, and they found comfort in that, a warmth and a camaraderie and a slight diminishing of fear.

If Ben knew about the new room allocation, he did not mention it.

On the last few days, they constantly discussed what they would do with the next instalment of the money, egging each other on with increasingly bizarre suggestions.

Ceci, who had barely given Stuart a thought in weeks, was determined to move out of Nicole's as soon as possible. However, in the event, when they arrived back in London and Ceci and Nicole made their way back to Nicole's, Chantal gave them both such a warm welcome that Ceci's resolve wavered. How miserable to live alone, she thought, when in this shabby flat there was constant friendly company.

Ceci could imagine her pathetic little routine if she was on her own, her sad little footsteps echoing back and forth in some tiny damp space. Toast and poorly executed meals for one and the hollow company of the television set.

Nicole had always said she should stay, for her it was a no-brainer, she repeatedly insisted on it.

"I will need to work or study or something eventually though." Ceci was concerned that Nicole believed that she would just be sitting at home watching Chantal constantly. Appealing as the prospect was, it was not realistic.

"No hurry!" laughed Nicole.

And Ceci acknowledged that, of course, there would be no hurry, as she didn't even know what she wanted to do yet. No more promo work after this tour, that was for sure.

It was the beginning of October and London was flirting with the onset of a wintry chill. As the girls lugged their suitcases back to their various abodes, they felt varying degrees of relief to be home relatively unscathed. Only Becky blithely anticipated the third tour and yet more money, only Becky did not feel threatened in any way.

Only three weeks until the third tour.

Nicole got a series of catwalk shows almost immediately.

Becky returned to her dance class and called her agency to inform them she was temporarily free. Her agent told her that there was quite a bit of work coming up and that she would be in touch.

Chantal was eager to show Ceci the bundle of university prospectuses that had arrived in her absence.

"I have been reading up on it," She informed Ceci with great seriousness, and if you don't have A-levels…"

"I don't have A-levels." Ceci sighed.

"Well, that's OK, because you can do this other qualification to get in, it explains it clearly here…" She flicked through one of the leaflets to show Ceci.

Chantal was so earnest and invested in the, in Ceci's eyes, unrealistic plan, that Ceci felt compelled to at least pretend to consider it seriously.

Emma, back in her damp little flat was greeted by her flatmates like a conquering hero. Maybe months ago, this would have moved her, her sentimental soul, but now she just reminded herself cynically that they were actors, actors acting, and right now they just perceived her as this great big cash machine.

Had she been able to share that thought with anyone at that moment, she would have been persuaded to think rationally perhaps and realise that it was not entirely fair, nor true. At some point, in the not too distant past, they had all been poor together, and they had been friendly with Emma then too, all the same.

"I am going to visit my family." She told the boys bluntly the following day. They must have noticed that Emma was behaving strangely towards them (Emma had always been strange, but not towards them, they had been under the impression that they were all in it together, a unit), and seemed hurt and bemused.

Emma did not appear to notice or care. She packed a bag and got on a train. Once on the train, she dozed against the rain splattered window, the fields smearing past in a blur of vibrant green. Still dopey at the other end, and starving, because she had not eaten since the previous day, she walked through the village to her childhood home, befuddled by the stillness and the quiet and besieged by the familiar smells and sounds.

"Emma!" Emma had let herself in with her old key and her mother stood there, looking prematurely elderly and aghast.

The Rivers and the Sea

Emma's brother had moved out by then and her father was out at work still, but her mother had retired out of the workforce early, crippled by chronic arthritis.

Emma knew this about her mother from her sporadic visits and phone calls, and yet, the two of them regarded each other, there in the small hallway, in a type of dumb, mutual shock. Emma's mother, previously always active and vital, was now reliant on a collection of walking aids. In the hallway, she was leaning heavily on a walking stick, one pale, meaty hand gripping it unsteadily. In a nylon pink cushioned dressing gown and with her grey hair escaping from a straggly bun, she bore no resemblance whatsoever to the photograph of the mother residing in Emma's memory.

Yet, in turn, there was Emma, always a mousey creature, who seemed to have retreated so far into herself that she appeared diminished. Yes, the hair was dyed a fashionable blonde (roots redone as instructed) and the glasses had long since been replaced by contact lenses, but her thinness was such that she appeared transparent almost. The very essence of her, always insubstantial even as a child, now seemed to be wavering on the brink of non-existence.

Emma's mother had not really known how to communicate with her daughter as a child and she certainly didn't know now.

"Well, you could certainly use some feeding up! Don't they have food in London? Come through…"

She hobbled ahead of her daughter into the kitchen which looked far more decrepit and worn than Emma remembered, yet there was a smell about it, a sourness, which recalled Emma immediately to afternoons after school, sitting alone at the table eating toast and doing her homework, bruising her feet in their thin grey socks against the cheap wooden legs whilst her brother kicked a football repetitively in the garden against one of the walls: BAM BAM BAM.

Eggs and toast and tea. Margarine. Full-fat milk. The biscuit tin with the face of the old Queen Mother smiling with the union jack background, the frilly yellow dusty curtains, framing the plastic window frame, decorative supposedly, for what?

All these things and the conversation which barely touched the sides. There was more loneliness in that somehow, despite the good intent behind it, the genuine, albeit dutiful, feeling of affection that was certainly there.

"How is the job then, the promotion job? Just t-shirts is it that you give out? Well paid, is it?"

Emma nodded dumbly. Maybe she should ask a question herself. It would have been the polite thing, she knew, and yet she lacked any energy for it. She didn't want to speak. One of the windows was propped open with a wedge of wood, the briny scent of the distant sea was carried through on the draught. It wasn't raining there, but the cold was always felt more harshly, the huge rush of the winds from the sea, the cheap homes, like theirs, huddled against the chill, in clusters. Identikit tiny rectangular gardens at the back, all with the same fences, rattling, sometimes tipping over.

"Will you go back to the waitressing after this promo job then?"

The enthusiasm had wilted in Emma's mum's voice.

"Yes," said Emma, "yes, I will."

"And that's how you heard about the promo job was it?" Her mum prompted. "From a girl at the waitressing?"

Did she know it was a lie? Emma wondered. Was her mother looking for reassurance? Even if she knew it was a lie, she wouldn't have known which part of it, or how deep the lie ran. It was all so remote and meaningless to her, Emma's life in the big city, like that of a character in a film she would never watch.

"Can I stay in my room for a few nights?" Asked Emma.

"Of course, love, you know you do not need to ask, this will always be your home."

And Emma felt a lump in her throat then and excused herself. In her room, which smelt so profoundly of childhood that the scent of it seemed to settle of Emma's skin, it engulfed her. She made her bed with the ancient worn sheets with the depiction of the cartoon characters that she had loved. She found all her old sketch books, her large black portfolio case which had been a Christmas present from her parents one year. There were seascapes still crammed in there, dog-eared, creased on thin paper, paintings that she had considered substandard and not for display.

The ones that she had found acceptable were still attached to the walls, a couple cheaply framed, but most with old blutack, as redundant now as hardened gum. The edges all peeling and curling away from the walls.

Emma studied her earlier work with a critical eye, with her innate self-deprecating insecurity. With her from London, she had brought her sketch book and her pencils and her paints too, just in case she got to that stage.

She sat at the tiny desk in her room, her knees crammed against the underside. She cleared the surface of all but paper and pencils.

She started to sketch another river.

By then they were flowing through all her dreams.

Sammy's Hair

Sammy had first bleached her hair when she was thirteen, the day after her mother's boyfriend, at the time, had crept into her room and started cuddling her.

At first, for the initial few minutes of pawing, she had naively thought he was being affectionate, she had had so little affection in her life, she struggled to identify it.

By the time she had successfully identified it as the opposite of affection, it was the beginning of the end of Sammy.

The cheap box dye burnt her scalp. Angry red welts rose up between the pale-yellow scorched strands of hair.

"It doesn't matter." Sammy said through gritted teeth.

Tracey who was with her at the time, who had warned her it was a bad idea, wondered at the reason for this dramatic act. It was only years later, when a similar but even worse thing occurred with another one of her mum's boyfriends, that Sammy confided in Tracey.

Tracey living a parallel, but much happier, situation to Sammy, had always been the cause of much secret envy. It is one thing to idolize the existence of unattainable situations, quite another to covet the ones down the road, which you witness on a daily basis, and have to pretend not to be jealous of, for the sake of friendship.

It was the fault of the boyfriends that Sammy was abused, not just one but two of them, and it would have been three, had the third not been so weakened by prolonged use of

heroin, that he had, one morning, just dropped dead. A flash of happiness had come to Sammy that morning, as unexpected as a sunbeam. 'Another one bites the dust…" she had hummed to herself all the way to school.

Her mother, albeit not the direct abuser, was, nevertheless the catalyst. Had she not brought the wretched losers into the flat and into Sammy's life, they would not have had the opportunity to touch her.

Sammy's mother was herself a woman with her own demons. By the time that Sammy was born, those demons had pretty much taken over.

Perhaps, she had given up and let them, but this is not her story and not her tale to tell.

She had not wanted a baby, but had learnt too late that she was pregnant with Sammy and a legal abortion was out of the question. She had tried to get rid of the foetus by all the dodgy means she could think of, except for the most brutal ones: gin and a hot bath, bashing herself in the stomach, smoking and drinking excessively, and yet, baby Sammy somehow clung on, a sucker for punishment even then.

After the birth in the hospital, the staff immediately noted Sammy's mother's complete and hostile indifference towards her baby and the family was placed on an 'at risk' register. That meant, at the time, that social workers were legally allowed to visit Sammy regularly for a welfare check. What they noted at the time was neglect, a disgraceful and cold disregard for the baby on the part of the mother. However, there was no physical abuse that they could see, and as social services were so over-stretched, only physical abuse was the catalyst for action. Reluctantly, therefore, they had to settle for observation only.

What they observed throughout the years caused the more tender-hearted social workers to cry on the way home. Until she was eligible for school, baby Sammy spent her days on the sofa in front of the TV eating crisps and white bread and chips. She was pasty and overweight and given to weird rashes and seemed to have a permanent cold, her small nose always encrusted with damp congealing snot. She was rarely washed and wore a filthy nappy until she was four, until, in fact, her social worker at the time, shouted and threatened her mother to teach her to use the toilet before she started school.

However, arguably worse than all of that, was the fact that baby Sammy was completely ignored. Nobody spoke to her from one day to the next, beyond barked, indifferent instructions. She learnt to speak from the television, but even so, obviously, the developmental delay was pronounced.

Sammy's primary school was full of children with developmental delay, mainly for similar reasons. Sammy was not exceptional. The teachers almost never saw Sammy's mother and, as the years passed, her disinterest towards Sammy's education was duly noted.

But there were many Sammys.

And just like all the other Sammys everywhere, she developed a hard, almost impenetrable shell, which did nothing but harden further, year on year.

Having Tracey as a friend, at least, kept a tiny part of her vulnerable and normal at least. Had it not been for Tracey, she would probably have turned to full-time violence long since, particularly after the men happened to her.

Inevitably dependant on minimum wage jobs when she left school, Sammy had decided, long since, that the only way out of poverty, and, ergo, the only way that she could leave her mother's flat was to find a man, better than the degenerates that she had encountered so far, to fund her life.

Promotion work had seemed to provide that possibility. Maybe not at the lowly end of it where Sammy was based, but she had optimistic hopes for advancement.

Until now. Something was off, she could sense it.

When Ben dropped them off after that second tour, Sammy felt a sudden, dramatic compulsion never to return to that car park or that van. The thought of doing it again brought a cold chill to her heart, that was how it felt.

Not because of the job itself, of course not. It was easy. It was money for nothing. There was something beyond it though, something waiting to pounce.

It was a wisp of a demon she could sense out of the corner of her eye.

Becky and the Dancing Audition

"Can you dance Becky? There's an audition, well a casting, in a few hours."

"What? I mean pardon?" Becky had just woken up, several days after the return to London. It was quite late in the morning and her parents were at work already, but she felt uncommonly exhausted. It had been the phone, in fact, that had roused her from the sort of sleep that felt like quicksand, and standing there in the hall, she felt the sticky pull of it still.

It was the first time her agent had asked such a question and she felt momentarily confused.

Hazily, she recalled the advice someone had given her once about people asking whether she could do things. Basically, just say yes and worry about it later, that had been the gist of it.

"Yes, yes I can, what is it?"

"Oh wonderful. I'll definitely put you forward, you have exactly the look that they want!"

"Yes, but what is it?"

"It's a series of television commercials with a trio of girls performing a dance routine, one white, one black, one Indian…Oh sorry, I didn't mean that to sound…" Her booker sounded panicked.

"It's fine, I'd love to go for it!" Becky's heart hammered within her as she took down the address of the casting. Her dancing was rudimentary at best.

Becky had learnt by experience that casting directors were drawn to the young and bubbly side of her. Becky was a happy girl, so it didn't take much to embrace that side of her persona. With make-up, she emphasized her enormous dark eyes. Her clothes and jewellery deliberately enhanced her petite and delicate frame.

In front of her bedroom mirror, she practised a few of the dance moves that she had recently learnt, and laughed self-deprecatingly at how uncoordinated and ungainly she looked.

She would just have to wing it, she knew. She had done so before. She grinned widely into the mirror and gave herself a corny thumbs up. She was ready.

The waiting room next to the studio where the casting was held looked reassuringly empty. There were only a few girls there, but they did, to be fair, look more like professional dancers than promo girls; lithe and flexible with the sort of underfed, razor-sharp cheekbone look that ballet dancers always seemed to have. Becky sighed. I'm here now, she thought to herself, no harm in trying.

The casting lady came through to usher in the next candidate and Becky realised that she recognised her. The lady had a chiffon scarf knotted around her neck, beneath which a snakelike scar was visible in increments. It took Becky a few moments to siphon through the various locations in which she might have spotted the woman and finally she realised.

 It had been at the casting and training day for the mystery product tour.

It was an uncalculated move on Becky's part to approach the lady and have a chat. Naturally friendly and gregarious, that was just the sort of thing that she would normally do.

Having ushered in the next girl, the lady dallied behind a desk, on which, Becky had already seen, was a list of girls and agencies. With a wide smile, Becky moved towards her.

"Hi! I don't know if you remember me? I'm one of the girls on tour promoting the mystery product. I believe you were at the casting?"

The woman regarded Becky with an unmistakable look of alarm. It was in her eyes, they widened and flickered as if Becky was approaching with a threat.

A heartbeat of silence.

"I don't work for them anymore. I…" The woman looked away and shook her head. "I can't talk about it."

"Oh!" Said Becky, taken aback by such a reaction to a simple greeting.

"You are still doing the tours?" The troubled eyes were on Becky again, an intense searching look. She had deep grey shadows under her eyes, panda-like.

"Erm… yes, we have finished the second and we are soon to do the third. Do you know what the product is?" Becky asked smiling.

The woman shook her head impatiently.

"It's not the product that's the problem, you don't have to worry about that."

"I wasn't worried, I…"

She laid a slim hand on Becky's arm, an older hand, a maze of veins etched on the back of it, like a collection of streams, all merging.

"And he's OK, is he? Your manager, your driver?" She shook her head again and looked around, a fleeting look of something that resembled fear.

Fear of what though? In the room there were just dancers.

"What about the drivers?" Asked Becky gently, "What is it that you are worried about?"

"I…" The woman shook her head again. "When they recruited the drivers, the managers, I realised…and …I can't, sorry, I can't talk to you, they might find out and then I'll lose this job as well, just be careful, please!" With that she fled out of the room in the opposite direction from which the girls had entered.

Becky was still ruminating on this puzzling exchange when another lady called her in to the audition. At least she had not had time to be nervous.

There was a desk with two people behind it and a stereo on top of it, and a woman with a leotard and legwarmers, stretching idly in front of it. Like the dancers in the waiting room, her hair was pulled back in a severe bun. The room has full-length mirrors covering one entire wall.

Becky felt heat gather through her body and sweat prickle and itch beneath her clothes.

The two people, one man and one woman smiled indifferently at Becky but the dancer lady seemed the least friendly. She informed Becky that she would perform a routine which she would expect Becky to pick up quickly and then repeat.

Becky swallowed rapidly but her throat was bone dry.

Without further ado, the music was switched on, a rousing pop tune, and the choreographer performed the dance routine, somehow managing to convey both skill and intense boredom simultaneously.

It was too difficult for Becky, certainly too difficult for her to pick up straight away, she realised that immediately. It wasn't something that you could wing. Had she had more time, she might have been able to get it, just about, but the point was, of course, that accomplished dancers were able to pick up moves straight away and Becky was not, and that was what they needed.

As Becky left the room and the casting, she looked for the older lady with the scarf, but she was not there. Another younger woman had taken her place.

On the way back home, Becky didn't think about her substandard dancing, she thought about what the woman had said and wondered what it meant.

Stuart

It was early afternoon on a Tuesday and Chantal was dozing on the sofa and Ceci was washing up in their tiny cramped kitchen when there was an aggressive banging on the front door. Ceci froze, a plate gripped tightly in one soapy hand.

It was not, after all that time, Stuart that she initially thought of. The estate was considered dangerous and nobody ever answered the door to knocks like that; it was common sense.

Nicole was out at a modelling job, but she had her own key, and had she forgotten it, she knew not to knock like that.

It was such a small flat that any significant movement within could easily be heard outside the front door and from the walkway in front of it. Mindful of that, Ceci tiptoed to the living room where the old lady was stirring, her expression as she roused herself, both pained and troubled. Chantal suffered from various arthritic aches and pains which she rarely complained about, but her facial expressions, Ceci had noticed, gave her away.

"What the devil is that racket?" She mumbled to Ceci, slowly adjusting her body in the recliner.

"We'll ignore it is what we'll do." With a plump hand and a gentle nod, she patted Ceci's own hand and Ceci only then realised that she herself was gripping at the edge of the old armchair, her fingers rigid and clawlike.

"Whoever it is, will go away, is the door bolted?"

"It is." Nicole always insisted that the bolts be drawn when she left and only pulled back when they were anticipating her return.

Chantal put the TV on with the sound down and the subtitles on, and within a short time, the banging stopped and Ceci, absorbed in some old-fashioned black and white film, almost managed to forget about it.

It was only hours later, when Nicole was due back and Ceci went to undo the bolts that she felt an inexplicable glimmer of unease. It was quiet out on the walkway in front of the flat and yet the silence seemed loaded in some way. But was there really someone still there, or was Ceci's imagination running wild?

The answer came soon enough and was unwelcome.

"Who are you and what the hell do you want?" Nicole's voice could be heard clearly and both Ceci and Chantal tensed immediately. Chantal bolted upright to the best of her ability and Ceci stood up and ran to the door.

"I know she's in there! I know she's living with you!"

It was Stuart's voice, it was unmistakeable, but how had he found her? Obviously, someone had told him, but who?

"I have no idea what you're talking about!" Nicole was employing her scary voice, "But you need to vacate this area immediately before I take action!"

Ceci stood trembling just inside the thick front door. She imagined she could hear Stuart breathe, thick and raspy and agitated. A few seconds later, footsteps could be heard retreating and a few minutes after that, Nicole unlocked the door. There was heavy black and purple make-up round her eyes and purple lipstick smeared over her full lips and she looked even scarier than usual.

"I don't know why you are worried about that boy, I could take him on anytime!" Was the first thing she said. "Seriously, why on earth were you with him? What was it that you saw in him?" She didn't look remotely worried, just perplexed and Ceci was somehow comforted by that; she was right, of course, what could Stuart actually do?

Still, it was one thing feeling brave with Nicole at home and quite another when she wasn't.

"How do you think he found me?"

"Well, I would have said via our agencies, but of course, we're not with the same one, so some convoluted detective work to be sure!"

"The mystery product people must have all our addresses, they post out the payslips."

The girls, standing in the tiny hallway still, looked at each other.

"It's not that deep." Nicole tried to smile reassuringly. "Let's think about the money instead, that always cheers us up!"

Ceci smiled tentatively. It was true, now that they had been paid twice, that none of the girls had ever been so rich, nor even dreamt that they would ever be so rich.

"But…" She couldn't let it go. "He was there all day, all day waiting…someone who could wait that long in the cold, he's not just going to give up!"

"Well then, I'll just have to have several words with him, won't I?" Nicole's eyes flickered in the dark hall and she flexed her fingers. "Look, I'm not working for the next few days, if he shows up again, I'll make sure he gets the message.

What the hell does he want, anyway? To drag you back to him!"

"I doubt it, he's seen the payslip, the first one anyway, he wants the money, for sure."

Ceci had, at least, managed to divert her second payslip to Nicole's flat.

"Let him try." Said Nicole.

Changing some small things

Sammy, late morning, sat at the kitchen table and stared at the second payslip which was sitting before her. Such an innocuous bit of paper with so much power. She couldn't help but grin every time she looked at it.

She knew she had to make sensible decisions with that quantity of cash.

This was, in many ways, Sammy's one big opportunity.

She calculated, sitting there in the murky stillness of the dirty kitchen, that it was enough, for sure, to move out and pay rent in either an average-sized studio somewhere or in some decent shared accommodation, for about six months without worrying about work.

The next tour would pay for nine months. The fourth for a year.

At the training day, they told the girls that they would review the situation after one year, but very likely that phase of the promotion for the mystery product would end there, and they would move on to the next phase.

The girls had not been told what that would be, ergo, Sammy thought then, as she had deduced at the time, that it would be unlikely to involve them.

She heard then the unpleasant guttural groans issuing from her mother's bedroom which always signified that she was waking. Sammy sighed. As always, she had no interest in seeing her mother, of seeing her stagger to the kitchen in a pungent hungover haze. They were like two hostile ships in that flat, who navigated around each other constantly, trying to leave the most amount of space between them as physically possible.

Had the council been willing to provide a flat for Sammy when she reached eighteen, she would have been out of there like a shot. Unfortunately, the council were cash-strapped and overwhelmed and no offer had been forthcoming.

Now, as Sammy retreated to her tiny bedroom, she realised that having enough money for rent and living expenses for a year was not enough, because after that year, she would be back to exactly what she had started with, having achieved nothing.

 No, she needed to take a leaf out of Ceci's book and get some further training for herself in something that she would find halfway tolerable and in which she could earn a living wage. Not shop work, because she hated that, and she was not literate enough for university…perhaps…hair? She had always had an interest, or make-up? She could train as a beautician perhaps?

Sammy sat on her bed and looked at her pale reflection in the mirror. Her extensions looked dry and ratty there is the unforgiving daylight streaming in at the window. They hung about her shoulders like twisted strands of dirty string.

 Enough, she decided. She grabbed a pair of scissors.

Ceci meanwhile was simultaneously relieved to have Nicole home, whilst also increasingly annoyed with herself for needing protection. There had always been a powerlessness about her, she acknowledged then, and with that realisation came a moderate self-disgust.

Back in the distant town of her childhood, it had been the same. A habit it had become, as one of the youngest, to depend on the eldest siblings, who had managed as best they could, poverty notwithstanding, with a kind of grim tenacity.

Vapid, Ceci, thought of herself then, weak. She was cowering in a kitchen in South London from a man really not that much bigger and on the other side of a fortified door.

What would he do, really? Beat her up? Unlikely. He wanted to intimidate her face to face, and the fear of that alone was keeping her in hiding.

Sod it.

She retrieved her jacket, a black puffy thing, from where it was hanging in the hall.

"I'm going out!" She called into the living room.

"Wait!" an anxious flurry of voices, and Nicole appeared, in the frayed tracksuit she habitually wore around the flat, towelling, unfashionable and old, her expression both puzzled and concerned.

"Where are you going? Give me a moment to get dressed, I'll come with you!"

"No!" Ceci shook her head fiercely against her own doubt and cowardice. "I can't keep being scared, I have to deal with him and I have to do it alone."

The Third Tour

It was the day before Halloween. A frigid rain had fallen on the carpark where they always gathered, and in the aftermath of it, a weak sun glimmered in the gritty puddles.

"You look different Sammy!" Nicole nodded approvingly.

"Thanks!"

Sammy did not know whether it was meant as a compliment or not, and yet she no longer cared. The extensions had gone. Her hair had been dyed a natural looking dark blonde and the fake eyelashes had been removed. She looked like a different girl, plainer yes, but sturdier somehow, less vulnerable. The jeans were the same and yet she wore her t-shirt untucked.

Ben did a doubletake and frowned.

"Not sure I like the new look. When you were employed, the idea was that you didn't change your appearance."

His own hair had grown out wiry and uneven. He had, since last seen, developed a chubbiness, a jowly look in profile, he looked somehow badly aged. Nicole nudged Ceci and nodded sagely. Addicts deteriorated quickly, she knew that.

"I must have missed that part of the training." Said Sammy, and Ben glared at her, at all of them and instructed them to get in the van.

By then almost all the purple question mark stickers had peeled off, only one on the back of the van remained.

"We are losing our identity." Muttered Nicole to herself with a sad smirk. It seemed the others hadn't noticed.

Standing in the wet carpark, with all the other groups around them, same as them and yet unknown, all boarding their vans with their managers, Emma had watched them thinking her own garbled thoughts, whilst Becky had watched them thinking about what the woman at the casting had inferred.

The managers, in particular, were of interest. She had tried to spot the way they interacted with each other, to see if they interacted at all. No, not visibly, but that didn't mean anything. They were busy in that car park, under that leaden sky, herding their sheep into the vans, their girls.

Their girls: well-paid, gullible.

There would have been other times, meetings in grimy pubs, Becky knew, she had overheard similar men, men like them, and their slimy exchanges, their inadequacies masked by brute force. They would boast to each other.

Look what I can do.

What goes on tour, stays on tour.

Boys will be boys.

Becky had never had to worry about those men before, they had never entered her orbit.

She shook her head to try and clear it and then they were all, once again, speeding down the motorway, as before, with the rock music blaring, staring at the back of Ben's meaty neck.

Becky had no proof, she knew. It was just a rumour. Maybe the casting lady had been sacked, maybe the veiled, the cryptic, accusation had been uttered in bitterness, malice.

There was no point saying anything to the others, thought Becky then.

A decision she would come to regret.

A distant town was their destination. It seemed to the girls, as they drove, that they were heading deeper and deeper into the murky grey sky, weighted heavily by the constant suggestion of rain.

"There will probably be a river." Muttered Emma to no one in particular, her tiny hands clutching each other, the bones of her knuckles like a child's backbone. In her suitcase, this time, concealed beneath her clothes, was her sketch pad, her preliminary drawings.

Becky, sitting next to Emma as she always did, no longer rolled her eyes, or automatically dismissed her inane ramblings. She stared, instead, out at the endless snaking river of motorway, the zooming cars like so many giant manic ants.

Nicole, Ceci, and Sammy in the back were silent but leaning into each other, their limbs partially touching. There was an unmistakeable solidarity between all of them now, Sammy no longer excluded.

Ceci had not told Nicole what had happened with Stuart, when she had inevitably been intercepted by him on the street outside the flat days before. Even her silence on that matter was part of Ceci's new strategy. She had to be independent and she had to fight her own battles.

Hours later, after dozing and numerous stops at service stations stinking of urine and bleach and chip fat, the lyrics of the rock ballads rebounding around their brains, they arrived at their hotel.

Immune now to the wonder of a five-star establishment, they emerged out of the van and shivered. It was far colder there than it was in London, a bitter wind howled through the car park of that hotel. They stretched and yawned and dragged their bags to the reception, pulling the sleeves of their jackets over their hands.

 The colours of the decor were the same, a muted magnolia. The smell was the same too; lavender, bleach, a hint of citrus. They must use the same air freshener in the entire chain, thought Ceci. She was just about to share the thought with Nicole, who was beside her, when there was a kind of strangled yelp from Emma.

"That creepy Peter bloke, he's there!"

They turned, not afraid yet, expecting it to be a fragment of Emma's feverish paranoia, but no. There was Peter, the shock of blond hair, blotchy skin in profile, in civilian garb, sitting at the bar which was just visible behind the reception desk.

The Cold Town

Fearful, all of them still at the reception desk, even without knowing exactly what there was to be afraid of, they glanced at each other. Ben, signing them in, had not apparently noticed Peter, nor had Peter, who was looking the other way, apparently noticed them.

As soon as Ben handed them their one key per room, they scurried away to the lifts. They had two rooms on the second floor next to each other, as usual.

"We should sleep together in the bigger room." Said Ceci as they stood outside their rooms in the hallway.

The others nodded.

"I wish we weren't so far away this time." Mumbled Becky, and the others nodded again.

"You are usually Miss Optimism," observed Nicole, "What happened?"

Becky, in her mind's eye, saw the tight worry-drawn features of the casting lady with the chiffon scarf, and grimaced.

If she said anything then, there would be hysteria on the part of Emma, she knew, and she, Becky, would be obliged to manage it.

"Nothing." She shrugged. "Just tired."

The lift they had just used pinged. Ben emerged, stomach first, stretched taut beneath the purple question mark on the white t-shirt.

"How lovely," He commented, his voice as cold as ever, "This time, we are all on the same floor."

None of the girls said anything, made any attempt to formulate any kind of polite response and that seemed to throw him.

"Cat got all your tongues?" He tried a dry laugh.

"Ha Ha." Said Nicole.

They waited until he had shut the door of his own room down the hall and then they all got into the one room together, without saying anything, dragging their small cases with them.

A nebulous dusk had darkened the low-lying sky and they switched on the bedside lamps only and the TV, from which canned laughter echoed. Sammy and Nicole lit cigarettes, both sitting on one of the bigger beds, Nicole with her long, lithe legs crossed, the hotel ashtray balanced perilously on her thigh. The smoke permeated through the air like a fog, the windows were shut. It was very warm, and the girls felt their bodies unfurl and relax. The goose bumps on their arms disappeared.

Ceci, a familiar cramping in the pit of her stomach, undid the button of her jeans and lay on her back on one of the beds on the beige chenille bedspread with Becky next to her, stretched out and sighing deeply.

Emma stood staring at the large cheaply framed print on the wall. A meadow and a couple of horses grazing.

"Horses." She mumbled to herself, seemingly dissatisfied, and then rummaged around in her case, on the floor, on the beige carpet, for her sketch pad.

"What could it mean?" Sammy's tone of voice contrasted then with the silly jolly voices from the TV (a gameshow).

"That Peter is here? Why would he be here?"

"Isn't he a manager of this hotel? Maybe that's why."

"Of that one branch, not of the whole chain."

"Are you sure? We may be over-thinking it…maybe it is the whole chain he is manager of and it is just a coincidence."

Becky's heart banged and bruised against her ribs and she thought of the time that Emma had told her she had seen him in a different town, and she, Becky had not believed her.

Emma did not speak then, but under the canned laughter, her pencil could be heard, scratching and etching her desperate thoughts onto the paper at the desk under the TV, her little head bent forward, one arm shielding her work.

At 7.30 they met in front of the van wearing jackets because it was freezing and a thick rain was hammering on the roofs of the cars and bouncing off. Everything was terribly wet.

"You can't wear the jackets in the venues." Said Ben.

He had told them that before, Ben was a stickler for the right uniform, they knew that, and yet the weather had never been this bad before.

They knew not to argue, just jumped in the van, huddled in their jackets still, their bags with the t-shirts warm on their laps. The rock music went on.

It wasn't so bad mostly. He would make them take their jackets off and leave them in the van, but then drop the girls close to the entrance of the pubs. It was in his interests too, or rather the interests of the brand, that the girls did not appear too bedraggled.

It was a quiet night in that town. The terrible weather would have kept the punters at home. With Ben safely in the van, the girls gave the t-shirts away with complete disregard for the official script.

"Would you like a t-shirt, here you are."

"Can I have another one love?"

"Sure."

"What about one for my brother at home?"

"OK, that's it though." The worried glance over the shoulder just in case.

"What is this product then?"
"We don't know."

"Oh, come on! You must do!"

"We don't know!" The girls would keep repeating. "They haven't told us!" We don't care, remained unsaid.

At the end of the night, damp and cold, they thawed out in the hotel room and grabbed the towels from the unused room before taking turns to have a shower. They were polite and mindful of each other like never before. On their passage through the hotel, they had kept a wary eye out for Peter, but he was nowhere to be seen.

Nevertheless, Nicole jammed a chair under the door handle of the room before they went to sleep, curled up around each other like kittens, damp still and overwarm.

Halloween

It was dry at least, the following day, although it was still freezing and the sky was a universal pale grey colour. Through the window, was the car park with their van parked in it, waiting. Beyond that, a field, slick and shiny with wet grass and mud.

The girls woke late into the thick warm fug of their shared room. Already, with the excess of bodies and the heat, it felt insulated, cocoon-like. Unwilling to get dressed yet, they ordered room service for breakfast.

"We should go for a walk or something." Nicole yawned an hour later, "Or we will never wake up."

"It's Halloween." Ceci commented.

"Oh yes. I wonder if they dress up here, if the kids go trick or treating?"

"I dunno, it's an American thing, so probably more common in London."

Nevertheless, even on their walk early that afternoon to the rundown town centre, evidence of Halloween was everywhere to be seen. Teenagers were stampeding and giggling through the high street wearing cheap plastic masks depicting the usual ghouls and ghosts and skeletons.

"Boo!" they would leap in front of the girls and yell at them.

"I guess, Halloween is a thing here too then." Observed Nicole, dryly.

"Well, it's not a very exciting place, I guess they need to get their kicks where they can."

On the way back to the hotel, through some quiet residential roads, they saw several much smaller children trick and treating. Their tiny hands were clutching orange buckets, their mothers with buggies and worry-etched faces trailing after them and beseeching them to be careful and to say thank you for the sweets.

"Do you want kids?" Sammy asked out loud. Ceci who was walking next to her presumed the question was meant for her, but behind her, Emma answered, her voice sombre.

"I'm not stable enough to have kids, I know that."

They all made polite noises of protest, but what she said had about it the ring of truth.

"I don't want them." Declared Sammy, "I would have no idea how to treat them."

"I think you pick it up, even if you've had bad role models." Commented Nicole. "I've had a great role model in my mum, and I'm not sure I want them either."

Ahead of them a bunch of slightly older kids darted across the road dressed as ghosts, their white sheets flapping behind them like the wings of giant birds.

"Do you think we'll meet each other when we are older with families and stuff. and be, like, surprised, how we've made it this far?" That was Emma, sadness in her voice.

"Sure, we will!" Becky squeezed her skinny shoulders, breakable she felt.

"We'll always remember each other." Said Sammy softly. "For one reason or other."

That evening most of the drinking establishments the girls visited with their t-shirts had gone to town with the Halloween decorations: spiders webs, skeletons dangling from the ceiling, ghosts, witches, fake blood, the works. If they had music, they also invariably featured a spooky Halloween soundtrack. Many of their customers were dressed up too, characters from horror films featured prominently.

"I'm beginning to feel underdressed." Muttered Nicole.

"At least we have our very own monster in the van!" Ceci chuckled.

It was true that Ben was in a foul mood, even more so than usual. His countenance, when he was bad-tempered did appear threatening, especially because of the bulk of him.

It was at the last pub that things suddenly, surprisingly, started to go wrong.

It was not a large establishment, nor filled with drunk youngsters. It was the sort of place that they rarely went, the sort of place the girls knew, by then, was certainly not home to their target demographic. In fact, walking into the unflattering light and the relative silence and the old toothless men slumped at the bar, the girls wondered why they were there. Ceci, the first in, turned and raised her eyebrows at the others.

Still, it was the last pub and the girls knew they just had to give out the last of their t-shirts and then they could relax. Their chilled bodies were already aching to snuggle up in their warm hotel room in their pyjamas and with each other in front of the TV.

Ceci had just finished giving out the t-shirts to a table of bemused middle-aged punters, when she turned to find herself surrounded by a group wearing head to toe skeleton costumes, their heads luminous skulls. They jeered and shouted and tried to grab her bag. Ceci held on and shouted loudly for help and Nicole leapt and lunged at them from the other corner of the pub.

At some point in the kerfuffle, Ben appeared and roared as did the barman, brandishing some kind of broom, and the skeletons scattered, the door of the pub banging as they dispersed into the night.

In the van, not minutes later, everyone panting with the residue of panic and hysteria, Ben asked them if they were grateful to him for rescuing them, and Ceci felt doubt arrive and hover over her.

 How strange, she thought, that a group of skeletons had descended on an old men's pub where no one was dressed up. How much stranger that those same skeletons had immediately targeted the promotion girls who were then 'rescued' by Ben, who statistically spent 99% of the time sitting on his arse in the van.

Before the Terrible Thing

Ceci didn't say anything to the others until they were safely in their room with the door shut, and the window too, in case their voices carried on the breeze.

"It had crossed my mind too." Nicole nodded. "He is engineering these incidents so that we are somehow grateful to him, so that we perceive him as our protector."

"You think he doesn't realise that we don't buy it?"

"Well, I guess we seem to at the time, and the ego is huge on these people. They think they're so clever."

"Have you seen that Peter creature since we arrived at the hotel?"

"No, why?"

"Last time there was an incident like this, he was around too."

"I don't know. He's creepy, but I don't think we should get too paranoid about him. He might well just be a type of travelling hotel manager." That was Becky.

Nicole was having none of it.

"What the fuck is a travelling hotel manager, Becky, seriously? You mark my words, there's something off about the two of them."

The next day and night were calm.

The venues held an air of exhaustion after the excesses of Halloween and the punters were civilised. Tatty strands of plastic spiders' webs still trailed about on the grubby floors of the pubs, forgotten smears of fake blood, artificially bright.

The next day they drove on to another town through a seemingly permanent horizon of low-lying rain clouds. This time it wasn't far, less than an hour away, and the hotel when they arrived was obviously part of the same chain, but smaller.

Unusually, it was not situated on the outskirts of the town, as it normally was, but within it, just behind the high street.

The girls' rooms were on a higher floor, albeit next to each other again, and from the window at the end of the corridor, a church spire was visible, a neon sign advertising a familiar brand of fast food, a snaking line of rooftops, Victorian terraces, lowly and cramped.

This time, Ben, his room on the same floor, spotted them all trying to enter the same room and interceded.

"What nonsense is this?" His face always got ruddier when he shouted, the spider veins on his nose more pronounced. They were crammed, with their bags, in the narrow hotel hallway, the smell of it so familiar by then, it was almost like home.

"The brand pays for you girls to use two rooms! Why the hell would you try to squeeze into one?"

The girls waited for Nicole, their unofficial spokesperson, to say something, but actually there was nothing she could say. What explanation could she possibly give that would make sense to a brute like him? That they felt safer together, that the girls didn't trust him? She couldn't say that.

She mumbled something feeble and ineffectual about wanting to hang out together as girls do, and Ben had scoffed and dismissed the very notion immediately.

"You'll be using both rooms from now on, I'm going to check…in fact…" He gestured impatiently at Becky and Emma. "You two, bring your bags here and come with me, bring your key."

Emma's eyes widened in total panic and Becky stared beseechingly at Nicole, but again, she was powerless to do anything.

"What are you doing?" She tried to ask him, her voice small and a bit frantic.

"It's none of your concern, is it?" His tone was icy, dismissive. He marched Becky and Emma ahead of him down the corridor and jabbed angrily at the lift button. The other three stood there impotent and helpless, watching.

"It's not a spectator sport, is it?" He barked. "Get into your room!"

Nicole, Ceci, and Sammy slumped on their beds, fully clothed, not bothering to unpack.

"He's doing it just out of spite." Said Ceci, undoing the top button of her jeans and sighing heavily.

"It's funny…" Sammy's voice was quiet, pensive. Somewhere a motorcycle roared, on another floor a vacuum cleaner buzzed.

 "At the beginning, before the tours started, he could have had me just by clicking his fingers and yet he wasn't interested."

"What was it that changed for you?" Nicole stood up and took off her jacket. She looked out of the window. From that angle, she could see part of the pedestrianised high street, some benches with old men slumped on them, pigeons. "What made you stop chasing him, I mean? Stop believing that finding a man, any man, was a solution?"

"I realised suddenly, after the money came. I realised I needed more of that, and I needed to earn it myself and it was that which would buy me freedom…men, those sorts of men are just a…kind of trap. You believe that's all you're good for and it becomes a…a…"

"Self-fulfilling prophecy."

"Yes…exactly that."

Their phone rang. Ceci picked it up. It was Becky. She sounded irate and in the background, Ceci could hear Emma sobbing.

"He's moved us to the second floor. The room right at the end of the corridor. The hotel receptionist seemed confused as to why he wanted to move us, watching Ben try to explain was…interesting…you could tell she thought he was nuts!"

"Arsehole. I'm guessing Emma is not taking it well?"

"She is not." Becky sighed. "I'll try to get her to draw, that seems to calm her down."

"What is she drawing?"

"Dunno, she says 'rivers,' but she won't let me see."

On the phone line, they both sighed heavily.

"At least we know he's on our floor not yours, that might cheer her up, keep telling her that."

At 7.30, they met at the van, as they always did, but Ben told them that the first few pubs were walking distance, 'if they didn't mind,' his voice thick with sarcasm. They were wearing jackets, with their t-shirt filled bags hoisted on their shoulders, and the girls waited for him to tell them to take the jackets off, as he usually did, but surprisingly he said nothing, just marched before them, leading the way.

Ben's own tight purple jeans were fastened beneath his round belly. From behind, they stretched unbecomingly across his massive thighs. He himself was wearing a black puffer jacket, which was probably why he couldn't say anything to the girls. The back of his thick neck looked mottled and raw.

The was a frigid quality to the wind which seemed to foretell snow. Subconsciously, the girls huddled together as much as they could, their shoulders rubbed against each other, their hips. They hid their hands inside the sleeves of their jackets, freezing fingers gripping the straps of the t-shirt bags.

The town centre pubs were quiet when the girls walked in, populated with a reserved crowd of tired office workers along with the usual collection of lonely old men. Three pubs there were along the high street, only the last had a bit more life to it, a younger crowd.

With no van to sit in, Ben sat at the bar in each place, moodily half-watching the girls. Self-conscious for the first time since they had started the job, the girls frantically struggled to recall the correct script to say to the punters, in case he overheard.

Having to do it by the book, meant they couldn't give away extra t-shirts as they usually did, and their bags were much fuller after the third pub than they would usually have been at that point in the evening. They glanced at each other nervously, fearful that Ben would notice, but if he did, he did not comment.

It was a relief to be told that the last pubs were a distance away and they would need the van, both for the warmth of it and for the fact that they would no longer be observed.

The relief was short lived.

The Disappearance

By the time the girls arrived at the last venue, a sprawling disco on three floors, they still had a fair few t-shirts to give away. As soon as Ben dropped them by the entrance, they rushed in, split up and got on with it.

The sooner they finished, the sooner they could go back to the hotel, that was their only objective.

After the wintry conditions outside, the stuffy humidity granted a temporary reprieve until that, too, caused a prickly discomfort in its own way. The girls sweated, their jeans stuck to them, Ceci's stomach bloated against the confines of the tight waistband. The strobe lights flickered. Visibility was limited. It was exhausting. The girls pushed their way through sticky, pulsating crowds, tried to talk against the roar of the dance music, no one could hear them.

It was their habit, in each venue, to either meet at the exit at a certain time or, at the final venue, to meet once they had given out all of their t-shirts.

One hour later, they were all standing at the exit, just inside it, next to an enormous bouncer, stoic and silent as a statue. All of them were there with their empty bags except for Sammy. They did not worry, at first, it was common for one person to take longer than the others at the end. As the minutes dragged, however, a low-lying panic started to set in and they started trying to work out where they had last seen her.

The discussion was fruitless. In a place like that, they almost never saw each other, and they all recalled clearly seeing Sammy only at the start when they had first entered the premises.

The bouncer, hovering over them whilst their heads were bent together talking, suddenly made a sound. They looked up at him startled. He was so quiet, they had almost forgotten he was there.

"You girls talking about a girl dressed like you? Chubby? Light hair?"

They nodded. "Yes! Have you seen her?" That was Nicole.

He nodded his huge head. "She left with that bloke you are all with. He came to get her about an hour ago."

They stared at him and then at each other.

"Are you sure?"

"Why?"

"Are you sure it was her?"

The bouncer seemed disinclined to answer questions but scoffed at the last one.

"Am I sure? How many other girls are dressed like you in this here club?"

The girls were dumbstruck for several minutes, in confused shock. Later, they would all agree that they knew it was bad, but didn't yet understand how or why.

Emma reached a hand out impulsively to grab Becky's arm.

"She might have felt ill, that must be it!" Becky looked at Emma as she tried to reassure them all.

"Did she look ill?" Becky turned to the bouncer who frowned and shrugged, clearly bored of the lot of them.

"I didn't look closely." He turned away to stare blatantly in the other direction.

"That must be it." Ceci nodded, trying to reassure herself, all of them.

"Come!" Nicole made a sweeping gesture as if to round them up and pointed outside towards the darkness of the car park. "He will know!"

The cold hit as soon as they were outside and the shock of it was a short-lived relief.

Ben was there in his van as he always was, the doors shut against the cold but the rock music bouncing through the metal frame. He unlocked the doors as he saw them approach.

Nicole threw open the door to the passenger side without getting in.

"Where's Sammy? Is she ill? Is she at the hotel?"

The music was so loud that it was unclear whether Ben had even heard her and yet he looked at her for what seemed like a strange intense length of time before replying, his eyes black and hard in the gloom and orange glow of the streetlights.

"You'll see her later." He said and turned and started the engine.

"What do you mean? Where is she?" Nicole's voice sounded higher, infused as it was with panic.

"Get in now." He said, facing the windscreen.

"No…We need…"

"GET IN!" He roared, "ALL OF YOU SHUT UP AND GET IN!"

They got in and clutched at each other. Ceci's stomach hurt so much she felt it was going to explode. Emma's teeth were chattering but she was gripping at Becky's arm trying to stop them.

They weren't even sure yet what they were afraid of.

In the hotel car park, Ben unlocked the doors of the van and let them out. He had not spoken during the drive, no one had. The girls had not even dared to whisper.

They bundled out as quickly as they could and rushed towards their rooms.

"Come in with us!" Hissed Nicole on the way in, "Quick before he sees!"

"Before who sees what?" Peter was standing with his back towards the reception desk, his smug slimy smile fixed onto his face.

"Oh fuck." Said Ceci.

Nicole said nothing to him, she ignored him completely and they all took her lead. They did not wait for the lift but ran up the four flights of stairs to Nicole, Ceci, and Sammy's room. They arrived stinking of sweat and fear, hoping but not actually believing that Sammy would be there, and of course, she was not.

Drink This

The girls barricaded the door. They huddled on the two bigger beds and stared at each other, their breathing erratic and uneven.

"I feel like I'm going to faint!" That was Emma.

"You are not going to faint." Becky, whose arm was already round her, pulled her close.

Nicole, wordlessly went to the mini bar, which was forbidden to them, and took out four small mini bottles of spirits at random. She distributed them on autopilot and they twisted the tiny lids off and knocked the liquid back, even Becky.

The burn of the liquor against the back of their throats was momentarily soothing and distracting.

They all sighed heavily.

"It might still be innocent."

"How can that be? You saw him, you heard him! Whatever this is, it's not 'innocent'!"

"But why Sammy? Why now?"

"Now, because…he…needed time to groom us, get us in position…"

"Sammy? I think it could have been any one of us, maybe he walked into that club and grabbed the first one he saw!"

Emma stared horrified.

Becky tightened her grip around her shoulders.

"Maybe Sammy made herself available at the start?" She suggested primly.

"NO!" Nicole shouted and they all jumped, their nerves on edge. "He is a predator, they…"

"They?"

"That Peter is definitely involved, probably others we've never seen!"

"Do you think it's something to do with the product?"

"No…it's…" Becky hesitated. It felt like adding fuel to the flames, but she had to tell them then. She realised with great clarity that it had been remiss of her not to be transparent with all she knew before. She told them about the casting lady with the scarf and what she had said.

"And you've been sitting on this!" Hissed Nicole, "Why? Didn't you think we deserved to know?"

All of them stared at Becky horrified.

Becky stammered, ashamed. "I…I didn't know if she was telling the truth. I thought she may have been sacked, had a grudge against them, and was making things up to be vindictive. I'm sorry…I…"

"OK, OK, we need to focus now, think carefully. The drivers. OK. A group of men, known to each other let's presume, somehow manage to get the job of managers, how?"

"They have a connection, a friend who is connected to the marketing, that man, the man who spoke at the training day, in the car park, he was the client wasn't he?"

There was silence whilst the girls cast their minds back, scrambled for faded images of the man.

"Maybe, but that's total supposition, we have no proof of that. Let's just say, for now, a group of men with nefarious motives manage to get jobs as driver/managers for high profile promo tours, why? What's the motivation?"

"Well, partly, the motivation will be the same as ours, the money. I'm thinking they get paid even more than us."

"OK, that's a given, but let's presume, there's a nastier motive…why? Why promo girls and not hookers?"

"Because it's a thrill, it's titillating, there's the risk of getting caught. Promo girls are, well they consider promo girls as a challenge, maybe? And that in itself…"

"They're creeps, we can't guess their motivation…they…"

There was a knock on the door, faint, and then a louder sound, as if a deadweight had fallen against it.

The girls stared at each other, their eyes huge, and Nicole leapt over, whispered loudly through the door.

"Sammy?"

"Yeah, let me in!"

Nicole removed the chair and opened the door. Sammy, still in her uniform but without her jacket or bag, was slumped in a semi-kneeling position in the hallway her face towards the floor, her hair damp and matted falling forward concealing it.

"He drugged me." She whispered and Nicole made sure that the hallway was clear and then gestured to Ceci to help her drag Sammy into the room.

They dragged her in and managed to manoeuvre her onto a bed, realising in doing so that she was also without her shoes, her white socks were blackened and filthy at the soles. Her eyes were shut and she kept them that way. Her make up was smudged across her face, her skin pale and clammy, her breathing uneven.

"Sammy?" Nicole bent close to her ear, but almost immediately her breathing deepened.

"She's asleep. We have to let her be now. Hopefully, she'll remember something useful when she wakes up. We should go to bed now."

"Are you kidding? How are we supposed to sleep now?"

"We need sleep, without sleep we are even weaker and more vulnerable." That was Becky.

"They drugged her." Nicole said, "Didn't you hear her in the hallway? There's little we can do against the sort of people who are willing to do that. Sleep is not going to cut it, but I agree with Becky, being exhausted and wired is not going to help us."

Photographs

Of course, the girls barely slept, rather dozed intermittently with their arms around each other. Nicole slept next to the inert figure of Sammy, checking on her breathing repeatedly like a mother would. There was a chemical smell emanating from Sammy, sharp and unpleasant, as well as the far more familiar pungent aromas of alcohol and weed.

The morning brought the overcast gloom of another dreary day. The fragments of colourless sky visible through the curtains were somehow fitting. The girls all stirred in increments, one after the other and yet Sammy remained deeply asleep.

"Are you sure she's OK?" They asked repeatedly, peering at her anxiously. Her skin was so pale that she appeared translucent, fragments of make-up smudged in places like dirt.

"She's still breathing." Nicole would check regularly. "They drugged her, who knows how long she'll be under."

They ordered breakfast via room service, for Sammy too, and they went all out, ordering as much as possible.

"The bastards can afford it," muttered Ceci, "We should take them for all we can get!"

"We can do better than scamming extra croissants." Nicole said grimly. "I can do better."

"What do you mean?" Ceci glanced sharply as Nicole.

Often, whilst staying at the flat with Nicole and Chantal, she had felt that there was something that she didn't know about Nicole that the other two didn't want to share, some deep secret. She could never exactly work out what it was, beyond it having something to do with the estate they lived on. It had further come to her attention, more than once, that Nicole barely had any friends on the estate. It was as if her and her environment co-existed in a kind of mutual apathy, which was very strange given that she had lived there all her life.

Chantal, too, had less friends than you would expect of such a friendly, kindly lady. She had Brenda and some church friends, but that was all.

Ceci had been too wrapped up in her own personal homeless plight to question the situation, and yet now…

"She's awake!"

It was true.

Sammy's eyes had opened slowly and she groaned.

"I feel ill."

"Don't move, just stay there, would you like a drink? We have juice?"

Ceci and Nicole propped Sammy's head up with an extra pillow and fed her juice through a straw as if she was an invalid.

Becky stayed further back and Emma was at the desk sketching. She didn't have her sketchbook there, it was in their room on the second floor. She was making do with hotel stationery and a biro. The sound of the pen scratching through the paper and against the grooves of the desk was irritating, but they let it go.

Emma needed the distraction.

Sammy drank a great deal of juice and then she swallowed painfully and gestured for them to take it away.

"They have photographs." Was the first thing she said.

"What?" all the girls jerked their heads towards her supine form like meerkats.

"Photographs of us naked, that night we got drunk on cocktails and felt ill, that's what that was! Those arseholes drugged us, came in, undressed us, and took pictures of us naked and they are using them to blackmail us, that's the intention…"

Sammy took a deep, painful breath then into the stunned silence that followed that little speech.

"All of us? Photos of all of us?" A small voice. Emma.

"I don't think so, no, you two weren't drinking the cocktails, remember Emma went up to her room? You're free, lucky you!" She groaned and closed her eyes again.

Nicole and Ceci looked at each other with an expression of pure horror. That meant…

"I've seen pictures of the three of us naked yes." Sammy confirmed with her eyes shut still. "Last night, what happened to me was a blur, fortunately, I don't want to remember, but I recall him talking about how they all loved the pics and showing them to me in the van. He said that if I didn't do what he wanted, the pics would go to everyone we knew, that they had loads of copies. I was sitting in the van and he made me drink lemonade laced with something bitter and then the next thing I recall is being in the hallway here in the hotel, everything hurting, everything still hurts…"

"How did he get you out of the club?"

"He came up and told me he needed a chat for just a few minutes outside."

"And you went?"

"Obviously, I didn't feel like I had a choice!"

"And then?"

"As I said he told me to sit in the van and he handed me photos. He put the overhead light on, but I didn't really understand what I was seeing, then I realised it was skin. I was looking at naked ladies. He said, 'look closely,' you know, with that nasty smirk he has, and I knew then that it was me and I recognised your hair Nicole and…and…"

Sammy was crying then, with her eyes closed and her face still pale and filthy with tears streaming down it pinging off her chin onto her t-shirt.

"He said…" She sobbed, "He said, "your type, I know your type and what they want…you are that sort, the filthy sort." He must be right because I feel so disgusting, so dirty…"

"How about a bath, Sammy, yeah? A lovely deep, soapy bath."

"Yup." She sobbed, "Please."

That day, the rest of it as it dragged on, felt as if they were suspended in time. They all, subconsciously or not, looked to Nicole to be the fixer, but none of them had the tools to cope with this, or even to know how to help Sammy.

With Sammy in the bath, they all huddled together, still in their night clothes.

"What about if we go to the police or to the organisers of the promotion?"

"They have pictures of us naked! We know about Ben and Peter, but there are other men too, we don't know how many. If Ben and Peter get arrested, which I'm sure, anyway, they'll somehow talk their way out of, even if they get those two, the others will send out the pictures…"

"But…" That was Becky.

"It's OK for you and Emma" Remarked Nicole dully. "They have nothing on you, you are free."

"I don't feel free." Said Emma in her bruised tight voice.

"You know what I mean, Emma!" Nicole felt irritation rise. "I understand that you have other problems, but you don't have this one, this huge, insurmountable one!"

She glowered at Emma, she couldn't help it.

Nicole was standing at the window, and spotted for the first time, from that viewpoint, the, now familiar, white billboard with the purple question mark.

"Was that always there?"

The others clustered around.

"No, I don't think so." Ceci shrugged. "Who cares? Those things are everywhere."

"So, we really don't believe the brand had anything to do with this?"

"No, I…no. Beyond not vetting the psychos they employ, maybe deliberately…"

"What happens now?"

"I'm thinking…" Said Nicole, slowly. "We are going to get revenge, but we also need to be sly about it and make sure those photos of us don't go anywhere."

"What shall we do then?"

"Nothing yet. We get through this tour, and then, at home, we plan."

"You don't think he'll try…"

"No. He knows we know now. I think he'll try again with me or Ceci but he'll wait until the next tour."

"Well, we won't go on the next tour obviously!"

"Yes, we will, because that is when we kill him."

Four Days

"That is some shit joke!"

"Who said I was joking?" Nicole shrugged drily and turned away, lighting a cigarette.

They were all smoking so much, even the girls who didn't normally smoke much, that the whole room was dense with it, a toxic fog.

"I can't believe we just have to carry on!"

"Yeah, we do, we have to work for Sammy too. We can't jeopardise getting paid. We can't let the bastards take that from us as well."

That night, at 7.30pm, they walked silently to the van, just the four of them of course, Sammy had remained in bed with strict instructions to jam the chair handle under the door when they had left.

"I can't believe we're doing this!" Emma kept repeating.

Nicole knew that she was the weakest link and kept staring over at her and frowning.

"Just four days" She muttered to Ceci who was close to her.

"If we just get through the next four days!"

Ceci's confidence in Nicole was wavering. In her opinion the stakes were too high. Since the revelation about the photographs, she had not stopped imagining them floating about the UK via the postal service. Her conservative family, albeit very distant from her both physically and psychologically, staring at her naked body over breakfast, not understanding what they were seeing. Her promotion agency,

Stuart. Oh God. Logically, she may have questioned as to how Ben and his sycophants would be able to get their hands on all the addresses, but just then it seemed like they were capable of anything, like some malicious gang of anti-heroes.

There was so much tension coiled up within them all, that it was almost an anti-climax the boring night that they had. When they saw Ben, knowing now, definitively, how evil he was, they almost expected him to look different, like a devil sprouting horns.

He did not, of course. He looked like the same bad-tempered brute as before.

No one spoke in the van. Ben did not mention Sammy and nor did the girls. He handed Nicole Sammy's bag, clearly implying that the four remaining girls were responsible for Sammy's share of work in her absence. Nicole divided Sammy's t-shirts between the four of them, silently.

They refused to look at Ben, deliberately turning their heads to stare out of the window. Ben dropped them off at the venues and once inside, they went into their routine like robots. He stayed in the van and the girls threw the t-shirts around with a grim abandon, not caring who got them, and not caring, in that instant, if they got into trouble because of it.

At the end of the night, they met up by the door of the venue they were in and were desperately relieved that all four of them were present.

They all wanted to believe that he would not try it again during that tour, but how did they know? It was by no means certain. Ceci and Nicole, in particular, were on tenterhooks, knowing that it was them that Ben had photographs of, and them that he would come for.

That night they all slept together once more, Nicole next to Sammy. She had stayed in bed all day dozing constantly and when they returned to the room that evening, she let them in, looking terribly dopey and pale, and then immediately went to sleep again.

They kept the lights down low, their voices as whispers.

"That's the type of sleep you have when you need to escape your thoughts." Emma said and, for once, they all understood what she was talking about.

"I don't think we can risk another location on this tour." Ceci had crawled over so that she was next to Nicole. Everyone else was asleep. "I think he'll try it again, at the next place, on me or you, he has a taste now and he knows we haven't reported it to anyone, what does he have to lose?"

"I don't know, I don't think so…" The fact of the matter was that Nicole's mind was in turmoil. She was itching for revenge. She wanted to hurt him and she had a definite plan which hinged on them, at least her, being on the next tour.

"If you could just hang on three more days…"

"It's not a question of hanging on!" Ceci felt a bit desperate. She didn't think Nicole realised how much danger they were in. "He could get at us any time!"

"What do you want to do?"

"I want to go to the police, here in this town, early tomorrow morning."

"OK, I'm not stopping you, but he'll say you've lost the plot and have no proof, even if you drag Sammy with you, he will say we are making it all up and the police will believe him, and then, to top it all, we won't get paid for this tour!"

"Is that it? Really? You're worried about not getting the money?" Ceci hissed.

"No! It's not about the money, not in that way, but not getting paid is also letting them win, don't you see that? Look, we need to sleep, let's see how you feel in the morning."

The Sketch of the River

The next morning Nicole was still adamant that they shouldn't go to the police and Ceci did not feel confident enough to take the initiative without her. Sammy was too weak and poorly and Becky and Emma had no skin in the game really, that's how Ceci felt.

Not only were they at far less risk, they were also unlikely to do anything without Nicole's say so.

At 11.30, they met to drive to the next town. Emma was clutching a roll of paper.

"Her drawing," Whispered Becky, "I'll get her to show you later."

Sammy walked very slowly to the van, between Ceci and Nicole, avoiding all eye contact with Ben and then sat in the very back and slumped against the window. Make-up less, her face looked pasty and sickly.

It was a two-hour drive, fortunately in a Southern direction. There was something reassuring about heading towards London, at least, and not even further away.

It was Emma who first spotted it. Clutching on tightly to her tube of paper, she was, as usual, wound up the tightest of them all and alert to every tiny turn of events.

She made sure she could not be seen in Ben's mirror and then whispered in Becky's ear. That was one great thing about the constant deafening rock music booming and echoing in the van; he could not hear them if they whispered to each other, it was impossible.

"He looks green, like he's going to throw up, look at him!"

Becky transmitted the message to Ceci and the clandestine Chinese whispers went round the van, until they all peered at him with furtive glances to confirm what they had heard.

"He does!" Nicole to Ceci, "He looks awful!"

"A bad batch of whatever crap he's snorting?"

They had just stopped at the third service station of the drive.

"No," Nicole shook her head decisively, "that wouldn't look like that. I've seen people…no…it's much more dramatic. If there's a bad batch, it's life threatening, people keel over, pass out, they certainly can't drive, not even erratically and badly like he does!"

"What do you think it is then? He does look like he wants to be sick!"

"It's all that evil in him, poisoning him." Muttered Emma.

"It'll be something common and garden," Whispered Nicole, "Food poisoning or flu maybe."

"Let's hope he's ill for three days, this could be really lucky for us!"

For the first time in many days, since before that awful night in the club when Sammy vanished, something like hope visited the van and fluttered over the girls.

If Ben was ill, he couldn't hurt them.

On the outskirts of the final town of that tour, in the hotel car park, Ben lurched out, bent over, and immediately vomited copiously just outside the van.

"Maybe he's been vomiting in the service stations on this drive." Commented Nicole, drily. "If that's the case, he'll be missing his fix, a double whammy!"

The girls had got out of the van as soon as he had unlocked it and started walking towards the reception without waiting for him. Behind them, crouched on the tarmac, Ben cut an undignified figure; bulbous with green-tinged skin, a watery pile of stringy vomit before him.

Nicole walked up to the reception desk confidently. She had seen Ben do it enough times.

"We're with the mystery promo tour." She informed the woman behind the desk. "We have three rooms booked. Two for us," She gestured towards the others, "and one for our driver who is puking in your car park. Please make sure that our rooms are as far from his as possible."

Sammy sniggered and the others smiled.

"Oh! I…" the woman looked flustered and stared worriedly at the paperwork before her. I think your manager has to sign off on the rooms, is he OK?"

"I hope not." Muttered Sammy, loud enough for them all to hear. She had perked up considerably since they had realised that Ben was not well, and that fact alone brought a tiny sliver of joy to all of them.

"What the fuck are you doing?" Ben roared behind them as he approached the reception desk. He tottered on his thick legs and lurched. He resembled, in that instant, some weakened or injured hideous beast, a hyena maybe.

They all dispersed as he approached, except for Nicole, who stood tall, elegant, and strong, her shoulders back, still in front of the desk.

The receptionist stared, shocked, her mouth hung slackly open.

"Sorry!" Said Nicole cheerfully smirking, "I was just trying to save you some time since you appear to be…poorly!"

Ben signed the proffered paperwork and threw the keys at Nicole, meaning for her to miss them, but she caught them deftly. The girls moved as quickly as they could to the lift to their rooms on the third floor. The receptionist had put Ben on the ground floor, overlooking the industrial bins.

"We have to take our small wins where we can." Said Ceci grinning.

The girls ignored the smaller room as usual, and all five snuggled into the larger one. They drew the curtains against the colourless freezing sky, jumped onto the beds and lit cigarettes.

"Let's see your sketch then Emma!" The others nodded and added their words of encouragement. Emma looked, as usual, just like a child cross-legged on the bed then, much younger than her years. She peered at them wide-eyed and a bit manic, through a curtain of knotty hair.

"I don't usually show my sketches to people, just my completed paintings…"
"We are not people!" Said Nicole in a deliberately solemn, fake voice, "We are your partners in crime." They all giggled, feeling a welcome, albeit temporary release of tension.

"OK then…" Emma unfurled the sketch with a sigh.

Well-executed and detailed, it depicted numerous small figures in a wild river, being hurled against the rocks and drowning, their faces contorted in agony.

Homeward Bound

"Is that supposed to be us?" asked Ceci.

Emma turned away, shrugged. "I don't know. I draw my dreams. That terrible river currently flows through all my dreams. It didn't use to have people in it but now it does, I see them all the time. I try to save them, but I can't. Sometimes I am one of them and trying to save myself."

"Deep." said Nicole sombrely.

"Bleak" nodded Becky, "But great on the artistic front!" She reassured Emma quickly, "There's some real talent there."

The others joined in with the praise. They didn't feel qualified to judge beyond acknowledging that the sketch had moved them, which seemed to be the point of art as they understood it.

In any case Emma was the most fragile of them all, they knew this intrinsically, and always needed to be chivvied along, and the sketch was a great distraction from their plight.

Although Emma wouldn't have seen it like that.

In her mind, the sketch was their plight.

The girls curled up on the beds, in the warm fug of cigarettes and cups of room service hot chocolate. They watched films and dozed, especially Sammy, who had fallen asleep almost immediately as soon as they entered the room.

Late in the afternoon, the phone rang and they all looked at it sharply and warily. Nicole picked up the receiver. Ben's deep voice sounded strangely fragile. He told Nicole that he had a nasty stomach bug, that he would not be able to accompany them that night. They should pick up the t-shirt bags from his room and target the pubs close to the hotel.

Nicole did a silly little dance as soon as she came off the phone.

"Yay!" she whooped, "Man down!"

"We just need him to stay down now." Said Ceci.

"Preferably on a permanent basis." Muttered Nicole.

Despite Ben's condition, Ceci still worried, she couldn't stop. She glanced at Sammy's sleeping form and saw that Emma was napping as well.

"Who else is in on this, do you think? All the other drivers? Some creepy network of men like Peter? Do you think there is a tie in with this hotel chain?"

"Not necessarily, we have only seen Peter."

"Just because…"

"Yeah, I know…but I feel like we would have spotted other dodgy hotel employees."

"What about the other drivers?"

"I'd say some but not all. How will we ever know, though? As far as I know, none of us talk to the girls in the other teams, I certainly don't."

Ceci shook her head too.

"I barely talk to anyone, you know that!"

"It's the nature of the business, the girls compete for jobs, they are rarely friends, the creeps are banking on that, also the shame of it keeping them quiet. No one wants to share the fact that there are naked pictures of them floating about!"

"We'll have much more time to think about it when we are at home and away from him. Here we are constantly on edge, too wound up to think it all through calmly."

The four of them, without Sammy again, passed by Ben's room at the designated time. He had lined their bags up (Sammy's too), in the corridor and his door was shut.

"Excellent, we don't even need to see the arsehole." Nicole divided Sammy's t-shirts between the four of them again and whistled a cheerful tune as they made their way outside. The others trailed behind.

"You are just like the pied piper!" laughed Becky.

They had asked the receptionist where the pubs were and she had pointed them out on the map.

The first one was by the side of a roundabout and on the edge of an industrial estate, an unpromising location. A square, grey dirty building with a bedraggled union jack displayed over the entrance.

Inside it was surprisingly full of youngish people with haggard, pale faces.

"Factory workers?" Whispered Ceci.

Nicole shrugged. "Who knows and who cares!"

 She put her bag down on the grubby floor and shouted:

"Anyone want a free t-shirt or two or three?"

Everyone laughed, the girls as well as, after a few moments of confusion, there was a literal stampede and after 20 minutes, barely any t-shirts remained.

"Are we not going to get into trouble?" Becky worried.

"Who's going to tell?" Nicole shrugged. "Give me your remaining t-shirts, I'll give them to the bar staff, they can wear them and give them to their friends too. That's great promotion right there!"

They walked back to the hotel after barely an hour, giggly and briefly elated, sneaking quickly past reception and the bar in case Ben was watching, or, God forbid, Peter popped up again. It was only much later that Nicole took their empty bags and dumped them outside Ben's room, in the corridor.

The next day and night were similar and Ben remained in his room. Sammy was physically stronger, but Nicole insisted that she stayed in their room and rested. There was a deep misery that had settled over her like a cloud, and much as the girls tried to cheer her up, her smiles were only ever superficial at best.

It was only on the final night that Ben called their room and told them he was driving them. Immediately, their spirits collectively plummeted and all optimism faded.

"He could get us tonight!" Ceci blurted out anguished.

"I really don't think so, he's been ill, let's presume he's still weak." Nicole tried to sound confident but her heart was clanging heavily in her chest.

"I'll come." Said Sammy.

"You will not!"

"Why not? I can help attack him if he tries…"

"He'll isolate us before he attacks, you know that!"

"We must make sure we're never alone."

Sammy stayed in the room and that night, in every pub, the girls made sure they were always with their pair; Becky and Emma, Ceci and Nicole, sticking together, like glue, like children holding hands in the face of a monstrous fear.

However, Ben did look sickly, weakened, his face drawn. He didn't look like he had the energy to grab one of them with brute force.

The next morning, the girls woke next to each other and sighed with relief.

Only the drive home to go. They had made it, more or less in one piece.

The Unspoken Thing

It was only when Ceci and Nicole were back in Nicole's flat in Vauxhall with the door heavily bolted that Ceci finally felt safe.

"I can't believe that I used to think Stuart was the worst thing that could happen to me!" She sighed heavily, shaking her head.

"Yeah, that was relatively recent too." Nicole chuckled drily.

They had both knelt over Chantal in her recliner and received a warm, sweaty welcoming hug.

She had greeted them both with equal enthusiasm, and a warmth blossomed in Ceci then, a thawing almost of the fear that now resided there.

It was weirdly hard to relax though, there was a twitchiness to their limbs, the adrenaline of the past few days coursing through them still.

It was hard to believe that they were now safe.

Nicole had always chain smoked, but since the night of the attack on Sammy, Ceci had started taking smoking seriously as well.

"You two are going to poison yourselves and take me with you!" Chantal complained constantly.

It was November in the estate, an unhappy time of year. A bitter wind howled through the poorly lit concrete walkways. People scurried like padded ants in cheap puffer jackets, dragging their scruffy guard dogs through neglected patches of grass.

It was never warm enough in the flat so the windows stayed shut. The fug of cigarette hovered constantly over their heads like a wispy mushroom cloud.

"Well, we all have to die sooner or later." Nicole muttered darkly.

"The idea is not to take others down with you!" Chantal barked and tutted.

Ceci had rarely seen her angry, but now she seemed agitated, glaring at the pair of them, her hands gripping tightly at the arms of her recliner.

"It's not just the excessive smoking with the two of you! I know there's something else going on, I'm not blind and I'm not stupid!" She turned to Ceci.

"Is it that Stuart creature again?"

"No. No, I confronted him months ago, that time he came here. I threatened him with the police. I think he'll leave us alone now."

Nicole raised an eyebrow at her. Ceci had never told her that.

"So, if not him, what? It must be something at work? You've come back, the pair of you, all wound up!"

Ceci glanced at Nicole who shook her head quickly, briefly.

Perhaps Chantal saw because she directed her infuriated gaze squarely onto Nicole.

"Is this similar to what happened before? Am I going to have to find out from Brenda, or some other well-meaning friend, about something that is happening right underneath my nose, huh Nicole?"

Nicole actually blushed. Ceci was momentarily surprised. She hadn't thought, until then, that it was even possible for Nicole to be embarrassed. It was only later, that Ceci struggled to identify the reason for the embarrassment.

Was Nicole ashamed of what she had done? Or was she just embarrassed that Ceci was about to find out?

"I see." Chantal nodded slowly, her mouth set in a grim line, "You have not told your friend! I thought that must be the case, all these months and no reference made!"

"Mum!" Ceci was shocked to see Nicole's huge eyes actually fill with tears. She had never seen that before either. There was something horrifying about watching someone who never cries, cry.

"I didn't tell her, because she didn't need to know!"

"And yet, now here we are! A similar situation!"

"It is not a similar situation at all, please trust me, you've got the wrong end of the stick, like completely, it is nothing like that situation…"

Silence settled briefly and uncomfortably. It was Nicole who broke it, with heavy reluctance.

"I'm going to tell Ceci now, mum, OK? Just to make you happy."

"Nothing about this is making me happy, believe me." Chantal's voice was sour. "When you've done that, both of you need to come and tell me about the current problem." She added firmly.

Nicole took Ceci by the wrist and pulled her over to the tiny room that they shared.

Nicole's palm was warm and sweaty, there was a dampness to her touch.

"Whatever happens, we can't tell my mum the truth about Ben!" Was the first thing she said.

"Yeah, I know, but I think we're going to have to tell her a half truth or something, she's not going to be happy with nothing."

"Yeah, OK." Silence. It was dark in that room, except for a faint light coming from the hallway, and Nicole turned on the small reading lamp. A tiny circle of orange light and then a faded gloom.

"You still have to tell me though…" Ceci prompted.

"OK" Nicole nodded and sighed.

Things We Are Capable Of

"I had a friend all through school, Sarah. We were friends all through primary and secondary. She lived in the block just over there…" Nicole waved her hand, gesturing vaguely, "On the estate with her mum and her dad, to start with anyway…"

Nicole lit a cigarette, without offering one to Ceci, and pulled the glass ashtray towards her. Her hand was shaking slightly, Ceci observed, and that shocked her too.

"My mum knew her mum, back then my mum was mobile, of course, she would be going out and about in the estate, visiting people. We were all friends is my point, when we were little especially, there was more of a community vibe."

Inhale, exhale. Ceci wanted a cigarette too, but didn't want to interrupt.

"When we were fifteen, Sarah and I started hanging out with a gang of boys and Sarah really fancied this one called Sean. The irony was that the others were all kind of harmless, a bit dippy, but Sean, no, not harmless. Sean fancied himself as a bit of a gangster, fool that he was. There's always been gang activity, drug related, on the estate. Back then, we are talking four years ago, give or take, it was heroin and crack, some pills…"

Inhale, exhale. Nicole rubbed her eyes.

"So, I didn't know Sean that well, but unbeknownst to me, Sarah had got together with him and they were officially an item. I was distracted by something, probably sport. I was in all the sports teams at school and forever being sent out on fixtures. It kept me out of trouble and also meant I didn't hang out with the others that much after school, when all the matches were being played etcetera.

However, it also meant, that I was out of the loop gossip-wise. In a relatively short period, not only had Sean and Sarah hooked up, but both of them were smoking weed and taking pills. Next time I saw them, they were agitated and wired.

Sean was going down the gang route, it was what he wanted, idiot that he was, and that was how they sucked in all the new recruits, by getting them hooked on drugs, various drugs, it didn't really matter which ones, whatever they had on hand at the time probably….I didn't care what he did, he wasn't my concern, but he was taking Sarah with him and that made my blood boil. Back in the day, we didn't 'grass', probably the kids still don't 'grass' to their parents about stuff they know. I wonder now how Sarah's mum didn't notice and if she noticed why she didn't react…but nothing happened.

The two of them got worse and then it was summer and all day, every day, they were out of it. Sean was running errands by then, for some of the leaders of the gangs. He was getting paid, but the money was all making its way back to the gangs because of all the drugs he and Sarah were buying.

I had a summer job, this was way before I even thought of modelling. It was in a shop, so I was busy during the days and didn't want to stay out all night either. I missed a lot of it, I missed seeing a lot of the deterioration in Sarah, I mean. Then one day in August, this skinny thing knocks on our door and my mum answers it, and I can tell by her voice that she is horrified.

"Sarah, is that you?"

Chantal had not seen Sarah up close for years, so the shock for her must have been much greater than it was for me.

She brought her into the living room and gave her food and drink, but Sarah was so out of it, her eyes were rolling back in her head, her limbs twitching. Her clothes were hanging off her. It was scary to see all of it, up close. She couldn't even speak clearly, she was mumbling and she could barely remember her words and…do you think you could get me a drink, my throat is dry?"

"Yup, sure!" Ceci scurried off quickly to get a glass of water.

Nicole took a big gulp and continued.

"So, more than anything else, my mum was furious, she was furious that Sarah's deteriorating state had not been picked up and addressed by her own mother, I don't remember if the father was there at the time, anyway. But she was also furious that I hadn't told her what was happening, and that is what she was referring to just now in the living room. Anyway, back then, what happened was that my mother pretty much took Sarah by the hand and marched her home to her own flat, wanting to show Sarah's own mother what was happening. Of course, when she got there, she realised that Sarah's mother had her own issues. She was depressive and spent her days slumped in front of the TV. Possibly the father had just left them, I don't recall. Maybe there was more to it, and something else wrong with her, but at the time, that was my understanding."

Nicole lit another cigarette, this time also waving the packet at Ceci, who gratefully took one, and sat close to Nicole on the bed in order to share the ashtray.

"I wasn't there, so I didn't see what my mum saw. I only know what she told me. So then, a few hours later, maybe less, Chantal was back here with Sarah."

"With Sarah?"

"Yes, at some point it had been decided that, on a temporary basis, my mum would be looking after Sarah, because her own mum was 'indisposed' was the word that they used. Chantal vowed that she would be stopping Sarah from hanging out with Sean or accessing drugs, but of course the two were one and the same, everyone had worked that out by then. It was during a period when my mum was not working, so basically, she acted as Sarah's jailer. I was allowed out to work and then had to come back to hang out with Sarah. Sarah was basically kept locked in our flat. She shared my room with me, just like you are now…"

We both took a moment to trace the confines of that tiny room.

"And…how did Sarah take that? Being grounded, I mean?"

"At first, she was so poorly and out of it that she barely noticed where she was, but then, a few days later, she was detoxing and withdrawing from whatever, and she got really agitated and kept trying to leave. She was forever trying to get to the front door or to the phone to call Sean, for what I don't know…he knew where she was. The gossip on the estate was rife. People knew that my own mother had taken in Sarah and people had their own thoughts on that…"

"Some people were against it?"

"Yeah, I guess…Chantal had a rep as being quite a busybody. I didn't realise at the time, I was too wrapped up in my own perspective, but people didn't think she should get involved, they thought she had gone too far…"

"What happened then?"

"It was September. School had started up but Sarah was still in our flat, not going to school. We were talking about it, I remember that, how to manage it, I mean her going in with me, me keeping an eye on her, that was the idea. The problem was that it was a mixed school, still is a mixed school and Sean was in it, anyway…"

Nicole stubbed out her cigarette and took a big sip of water.

"Wow, I'm exhausted!"

Ceci didn't say anything. She wanted to know what happened.

"It never got to that…to Sarah going back to school, I mean, because Sean came round to the flat one evening. He was high on something and banging on the door. I was in the bathroom, my mum was cooking, but Sarah managed to get to the front door and open it and he grabbed her and started pulling her out with him, not forcing her, because she wanted to go. It turned out that they had been chatting on the phone, unbeknownst to anyone, that they had planned it all. Me and my mum rushed out as soon as we realised, and she grabbed Sarah and I pushed Sean to get him away, and he fell backwards, tripped on something, maybe Sarah's feet, maybe his own, maybe something else…anyway he fell back, like a felled tree, straight back, and hit his head on the concrete floor of the walkway and…not immediately but a few hours later…he died."

"He…what?"

Ceci thought she must have misheard.

"He was totally out of it, totally uncoordinated, he tripped and hit his head and died."

"Oh! So, it was an accident?"

"It was, but Sarah told everyone I pushed him so…"

"But you didn't mean to kill him."

"No, but I did mean him harm, so."

"So, that's why you don't have many friends on the estate?"

"Yup, honour amongst thieves and all that." Nicole's voice was thick with bitterness.

"The gangs are weirdly protected, or their families are…one way or another, my mum and I came out of it badly. Although I never got charged with anything fortunately, they ruled it an accidental death."

"What happened to Sarah?"

"Sarah and her mother moved practically overnight, out of the estate and out of the city as far as I know. About a year after that my mum had her stroke and that's where we are, and that is why people don't like me here."

Emma and the River

As soon as Ben opened the doors of the van in the carpark in South London, Emma silently waved goodbye to the others and bolted with her small tatty case and her latest sketch of the river rolled tightly beneath one arm. She cut a diminutive figure, scurrying away, her thick black jacket enveloping her entirely, like the shell of a turtle. Her tiny blonde head bobbed along like an unexpected beacon against the grizzly sky.

Back at the flat she shared with the boys, the smell of damp seemed ever more pervasive. It was an assault to all her senses as soon as she unlocked the front door. The revolting odour seemed to creep stealthily across her skin. She knew that it clung to all their clothes constantly.

There was no one there and Emma did not unpack her case. Instead, she went searching for another, bigger, case that she also owned and which she had lent to Adam months ago. The flat being miniscule, it took barely five minutes for her to locate it. It was shoved underneath his own bed. Unsurprisingly, attuned as she was to the slovenly nature of the two boys, good care had not been taken of it. It was dusty and grubby and sticky with the residue of some liquid which had clearly been spilt on it at some point.

Sighing heavily, but in a hurry to leave before anyone returned to the flat, Emma dragged the case to her room, flipped it open on her bed, and started stuffing it with all her belongings. Her clothes were hurled in with careless abandon, but with her sketches she took great, diligent care, removing them painstakingly from the walls and rolling them neatly into cylinders.

It was only when she glimpsed her modelling portfolio on her chest of drawers that her resolve to leave quickly and invisibly wavered. She knew she couldn't take it with her and neither could she leave it there where anyone could get their hands on it. She would have to dispose of it in a definitive way before she left London.

Emma started to panic as she was wont to do. She sweated profusely and her skin prickled and itched beneath her clothes. She made herself perch on the bed and breathe and then lit a cigarette with trembling hands, stubbing the ash out into a saucer onto the floor.

One thing at a time, she told herself. If her flatmates walked in on her leaving, so be it. She would cross that bridge when she came to it.

She put the portfolio in a plastic bag, put her jacket back on and left the flat. She had a vague idea that she would walk around until she found somewhere to dump it. She thought of a bin, but then realised it could easily be unearthed. Nothing else sprang to mind, and then she pictured clearly the drowning figures in her latest sketch.

She headed towards the River Thames.

Accessible parts of the Thames were not very close to where Emma lived and, being sensible, she decided to take a bus. She was nervous enough, certainly, to keep walking in a kind of manic haze, but physically, she lacked the fitness, the strength.

Deep down, she knew that.

Like a normal person, she travelled on the bus, her portfolio in a supermarket bag on her lap. How many times, she wondered, had she taken similar journeys with her make-up on, her portfolio proudly carried under one arm to this casting or to see that photographer?

Now she was thinking of where she could get the stones to weigh it down and drown it.

It was November and freezing cold. There was barely anyone in the strip of parkland that bordered on the River Thames. A homeless man had built himself a cardboard tent balanced precariously on part of a bench, an elderly woman with her tatty belongings in a shopping trolley manoeuvred down the path singing Irish ballads in a thin voice. Boys on bikes, their faces covered with scarves zoomed by so fast that their figures blurred.

Emma, gloveless fingers numb with the cold, walked slowly along the edges of the park where the shrubs were, the hibernating plants, looking for biggish stones. Gulls circled and squawked overhead and sometimes swooped down onto the wet lawn, huge up close, and fearless.

She placed the muddy stones she found inside the plastic bag with her portfolio, all those glossy photographs, many of which had cost her, money, or sanity or both. She did not care about the dirt on her hands or under her nails.

When Emma thought she had accumulated enough stones, she walked to the railings which overlooked the murky swirling river and contemplated the depth of it. It was impossible to tell. Emma, despite growing up near the sea, had a poor understanding of tides. The river would be deepest in the middle, she knew that much. There was no way that she could possibly throw the plastic bag that far. She nodded to herself, in silent agreement with herself, and looked up and down. There were two bridges visible, both had a pedestrian walkway, both a good distance away. She sighed heavily to herself.

She had started and now she had to finish.

It was hours later that Emma returned to the flat, frozen to the core, and speechless with exhaustion. The boys were both home by then and had spotted her suitcase open on her bed, the blank spaces on the ruined walls which her paintings had covered. They hopped around agitated, angry, worried, but knowing they had to be careful not to antagonise Emma and scare her.

They had agreed that Adam would speak to her.

"Where are you going? You know we can't afford the rent without you?" Adam's tone was wheedling; he couldn't help it.

Emma shook her head in reply, slumped down on the bed next to her suitcase and lit a cigarette with trembling fingers.

"Shall I make you a cup of tea?"

Emma nodded. Adam made her a cup of tea, realised that she was not amenable to discussion and left her alone.

There was nothing that they could say to change her mind in any case.

Emma slept that night, curled up next to the suitcase on the bed. There was no space to put it on the floor. She slept with her old duvet bunched up around her. She would leave her scent on it and gift it to the boys, (by abandoning it there), who would hang onto it.

For years, strangers would then imbue it with their scent; it would rarely be washed.

The next morning, at dawn, whilst the boys slept, Emma left, lugging her two suitcases. She got a taxi to the train station. It was still dark outside. London was at its wintry best before the indifferent crowds and the gritty dirt were exposed by the luminous grey winter light.

Emma took the first train home.

Sammy

Of course, Sammy was never going back to promotions.

Her body would remember this trauma like it remembered all the other preceding ones. It would hold it within.

In the van, all the way home, she had glanced at Ben periodically, at his meaty profile. He still looked greenish and peaky. She had wished that there was some way for him to die suddenly, without the girls being injured, just fade away and evaporate.

Ever since the night he had taken her to the room with the other men in it, she had been imagining ways that he could die. The memory of that night was still a fuzzy blur, and she didn't want to unblur it. It was the sharpness of pain that she recalled periodically, the cold against her naked flesh, the hostility, the pungent stench of sweat and aftershave, the desperate desire for her own self to dissolve, while they grabbed and pawed at her, her own powerlessness.

Never again.

Once back in the flat with her mother, after a couple of days, they had a rare conversation. Speaking to her mother, throughout her life, had always felt like being forced to chat to a stranger whom you didn't like the look of and whom you had nothing in common with.

Sammy had not looked properly at her mother in months, and the pasty-faced woman that now sat opposite her at the kitchen table seemed like some random person you might bump into periodically at the local supermarket. She had not become any more friendly, there was still a hostility etched permanently on her face, her thin lips downturned. However, she had mellowed in recent years. She no longer shouted as much or as loudly as she used to, or as consistently and maniacally.

Of course, it was a given that she looked far older than she should have done, with her stringy bleached hair and badly drawn on eyebrows, her skin deep etched with years of drug and alcohol abuse.

"Making a pretty penny, are you?"

Sammy had never told her mother how much the mystery promo was paying her and now she shrugged vaguely. Neither did she have to tell her mother that she was leaving a well-paid promo job. Her mother had never known how long it was supposed to last.

"I'm thinking of doing a beautician course. I've heard that you can do one in a couple of months."

Tracey had found that information out for her and had called her immediately to tell her, as soon as she knew she was home. Sammy had not told Tracey about what had happened. She hadn't even yet told her she was quitting the promo work. Tracey had found that information for her out of kindness. If Sammy thought about the fact of that too deeply, she wanted to cry.

"Right, that's a good idea I guess." Said her mother doubtfully. "Lots of them about though, beauticians I mean."

"After I've done it, I'll move out."

"Seems about time," Said her mother. "Find yourself a bloke."

If that's the solution, thought Sammy bitterly then, how come it never worked for you?

She didn't say anything though. She still had to cohabit with the woman for the foreseeable future.

In the car on the way back, the girls had whispered that they would be in touch by phone, that they could all meet up and plan revenge on Ben, on Peter, on all of them.

Fighting words and sentiment, but now that Sammy was back in London, albeit in the same room where other bad stuff had taken place, she found that she did not want to think about any of it anymore, she wanted to reinvent herself completely. She literally wanted to pretend to herself that she was someone new; she wanted to shed her skin.

Yes, she wanted revenge, but the desire to pretend that nothing had happened was struggling to outweigh the desire for action.

She wasn't sure the two desires could be reconciled.

She phoned the number Tracey had found for her and spoke to an enthusiastic lady who said she would be happy to have Sammy on board. She found out that the beautician course would take two months and start in January, after which she would be qualified to perform all of the basic treatments and she could start looking for work.

Until then, the helpful lady suggested, she could go to the library and do some research. There were, she said, plenty of useful books.

It was the middle of November. Sammy went to the library and got herself a library card. There was something soothing about the library. She could not recall the last time she had been in one. She had a vague recollection of primary school trips, all the kids jostling and mucking about while a serious-looking lady tried to sell them on the merits of books.

It was only now, too late, that Sammy saw the point.

She wished she had seen it sooner; the library was a sanctuary of sorts. Yes, there was an odour to it, elderly unwashed people occupied cheap armchairs there all day, out of loneliness, probably. But mainly, there was a sense of tranquillity, of order and diligence.

Sammy took to hanging out there frequently. Sometimes, she took notes from one of the beautician textbooks sitting at a long table with various students and sometimes she just read a mystery or a thriller.

She preferred the ones which featured revenge.

Becky and the Meeting

Becky didn't know what to do, she just didn't know.

Just like for the other girls, the money from the mystery promo tour had become an addiction. Perhaps her family set up was such that she did not need it quite as much as the others did, but it was great to have, and paid for the classes which she considered, by then, pretty essential for her future acting career.

Furthermore, the money somehow proved, to her parents, that Becky was right in choosing her unusual career, that she could, potentially, stand on her own two feet.

Although obviously promo work was not acting, not even close. There was no pretending it was, she could not fool her parents any more than she could fool herself. It wasn't even a step towards acting, it had as much to do with acting as waitressing did. Unless one counted the fact that other promo girls were often wannabe actors too, or wannabe models, dancers, artists. Wannabe something else, anyway.

Furthermore, thinking about what had happened to Sammy, made Becky's skin crawl. It was all so grubby, so sordid, so far from anything that Becky had ever been exposed to before in what was, essentially, a very pampered middle-class upbringing.

Becky hadn't even realised that things like that actually happened to real people, outside the pages of fiction books.

So, given that, almost certainly, she was not a viable target and therefore not in danger, should she go on another tour and receive another enormous pay check? Or should she leave now?

There was also the very real possibility that Nicole and Ceci would try to get revenge on Ben on the next tour. That could get extremely messy. Did Becky want to get involved?

Her sister, Aalia, after an indecisive period during her A-levels and an extended gap year, had recently decided to study economics at university, about which their parents were evidently overjoyed.

Meanwhile, there seemed to be an ever-deepening chasm between Becky's parents hopes for her life and the way it was panning out in reality, with particular reference to the shady characters that she was now exposed to.

Thinking about it was depressing. It was somehow even worse that they didn't suspect any of it.

Becky called her acting agency, but there was nothing going. In November, everyone always said things would pick up in the new year, and for some people they probably would, but for some they probably wouldn't.

Becky stared moodily out of her bedroom window at the bare branches of trees swaying in the garden.

The main problem was, that if she abandoned acting, what on earth was she going to do? She wasn't remotely interested in anything else.

A few days later, when Nicole rang to arrange the meeting that they had discussed having in order to plan the revenge on Ben, Becky thought that she may as well go along. Apart from her dancing classes, she had nothing else to do, no auditions or castings to attend, and she was sick of hearing about Aalia's new academic career.

It hadn't even started yet, and Becky was already over it.

Also, she missed the girls. She had become so used to them, so accustomed to their mannerisms and their smells, their turns of phrase. Sometimes, nowadays, she felt as if she knew them better than she did her own family. Already she knew that the lack of Emma's twitchy presence beside her would be an absence that would gnaw at her. Even Sammy would be missed, and she was the one that Becky had always felt she had the least in common with.

The girls met in a café in Soho. It was the sort of place that served overpriced drinks, but you could spend the day there quite happily, watching the sort of people that you would never see in the small towns or the suburbs.

Nicole and Ceci were already sitting at a small table by the window and Becky, when she entered, grabbed a plastic chair, and dragged it over to squeeze in. So rammed were the girls there, that their knees were touching and there was a familiarity in that too.

However, Nicole and Ceci looked different in Becky's eyes in some indefinable way. It wasn't that they were wearing 'civilian' clothes, on the tour, they spent the days wearing their own clothes after all. There was something else, some spark to them that had been lacking on tour. When Ben was there, they cowered in his shadow, even Nicole, which Becky would never have believed. Yet now it was obvious. Alone and away from all that, they were tough and sharp and almost…dangerous.

"He's an addict, of course you know that?" Nicole was saying then.

"Erm yes, I guess."

Becky did know that without understanding the precise details of it. You would have to be a blind fool to be able to ignore all the obviously unnecessary toilet stops enroute to all the destinations and Ben's violent mood swings.

"That's going to be how we get him!" Ceci leant forward earnestly.

Becky considered then how all that time spent with Nicole had hardened Ceci. When Becky had first met her, she had seemed ordinary, naïve almost, unfashionable certainly. Now she looked cool, edgy. She was sporting the right make-up, the right clothes. She no longer looked as if she came from some tiny nowhere town.

Even the way she smoked now looked sophisticated.

"How will we get him? I don't understand!" Becky asked, baffled.

Nicole and Ceci glanced at each other, they clearly had their own sign language thing going on from which Becky was excluded.

She felt a sudden, unexpected flash of anger.

"Look, if I'm going to be there, which I am not sure about at the moment, I'm going to have to know exactly what's going on! You can't be keeping secrets from me, certainly not secrets as big as this!"

That was when they told her.

The Leader of the Pack

After the story was told, Nicole was exhausted, but so was Ceci. The recounting of it had been exhausting but so had the listening.

"The gangs weren't happy with me of course. I killed one of their minions, after all. But strangely they have always left me alone, it is almost like there is a grudging respect there. It may come in useful now…"

"What do you mean?" Ceci's brain was still reeling, trying to process all the details.

"Come on! Let's tell my mother something to keep her off our backs." Nicole jumped up abruptly.

"What?" Ceci panicked. She didn't want to lie to Chantal, but couldn't imagine telling anyone the truth.

"We'll mention the lads surrounding me and taking my bag, the set-up, as I am now sure it was…"

"Will she buy it?" Asked Ceci doubtfully.

"She'll have to, we'll have to be convincing is all."

"Now you know all of it, do you?" Chantal turned to study Ceci, grim faced, when they returned to the living room.

"It was a terrible time," She shook her head heavily, "With long-standing repercussions. We, particularly Nicole, have been isolated from the community since, you may have noticed, Ceci, how we have few friends here."

"It's not that great a community, to be fair mum."

"It was good for me! Your generation, not so much, all the drugs, I don't know." She sighed deeply, with great sadness.

"Anyway," She looked up suddenly, sharply, "If anything else untoward is happening, I need to know!"

"Well…there was this one thing, mum…" Ceci watched, keeping her face neutral, as Nicole recounted the drama of the episodes when she had been surrounded by the youths in the pubs.

"Funny how they always pick you." Commented Chantal, frowning.

"Yes, I wonder why?" Nicole did look genuinely curious.

"Maybe it's a technique to bring down the one who looks strongest!" Ceci blurted out and the other two stared at her.

Nicole nodded slowly.

"Yeah, it'll be something like that."

Later, in the bedroom with the door shut, Nicole told Ceci her plan and Ceci swallowed nervously. It seemed kind of precarious and hinged on many variables, but Ceci herself couldn't think of an alternative.

"Maybe, we should just hand in our notice?"

"And let him get away with it? Are you mad?"

"The police?" Ceci asked feebly. They had been through this already. Nicole dismissed this with a wave.

"It'll be his word against ours. He'll say we're lying, they'll believe him and he'll still have the photographs."

"Literally, whatever we do now, those photographs will remain out there, because we know it's not just him." Said Ceci miserably.

"I know, that is why we need to cut off the head of the snake."

"I just think, there's so much that could go wrong…"

"There's no alternative! We've been through it and been through it!" Nicole inhaled the smoke from her cigarette impatiently.

"And anyway, it's me who is taking on the initial risk, I've got to get hold of the gear, the doctored gear no less!"

It took a week and Ceci didn't want to ask much about the process. She didn't want to be implicated, which was absurd, of course, because she was already implicated.

"Are you sure about this?" She ventured once.

Nicole was counting out notes onto the blanket on her bed, a cigarette held at the side of her mouth.

"Shush! Counting" And then a bit later, "Yes, it's costing loads extra because I told him to doctor it and he said he didn't want to…didn't want it traced…"

"How would it be traced?"

"Exactly. We'll be miles away in some hick town. I told him that."

"But he was happy to deal with you?"

"Not happy it was me and not happy that I asked him to add the fentanyl, but they are always happy about the money, those people, always."

Nicole put the stack of notes in an envelope. She jumped up and put her trainers on.

It was early evening but dark outside.

"No time like the present!"

"Really?" Ceci peered through the window doubtfully, "Do you want me to come with you?"

"Absolutely not! You look too innocent, no offence. The deal will be off immediately if they spot you."

The Fourth Tour; into the Lion's Mouth

It was December the ninth and did not yet feel remotely Christmassy. Bright blue vacant sky, freezing wind.

The little baggy of dodgy white powder felt like it was burning hot in the pocket of Ceci's purple jeans. The stress had been bloating her stomach since the night before, when she had lain awake for hours listening to Nicole snore lightly.

At least one of us can sleep, she had thought with a twinge of resentment. She understood the logic behind her being the one to carry the contraband. If Ben had his eye on anyone, it would be Nicole, not her. Yet, she realised then, with great clarity, that she was not cut out for a life of crime.

Her stress levels were through the roof.

"Well, well, well!" Exclaimed Ben when Nicole, Becky and Ceci walked across the car park towards him. "You lot must be gluttons for punishment. I was sure you would have given it up by now!" His tone was cold and hostile. Standing there, solidly, his feet planted wide apart, he looked as bullish and threatening as ever.

He wasn't even bothering to make an effort to pretend to be friendly for the two new girls who were replacing Sammy and Emma. They were standing, shivering to one side looking very apprehensive, as well they might.

One was blonde, one was dark. They introduced themselves nervously to the others as Sharon and Helga as they all climbed in to the van.

"What's it like?" Sharon, the blonde whispered anxiously, as they started driving and the rock music started up.

"It's fine!" Becky tried to smile reassuringly, "The money is excellent!"

"Why is it so cold in here?"

"He doesn't like to use the heating, don't worry, you'll get used to it."

Sharon looked at Becky as if she was mad.

The 'old' girls had anticipated that Sammy and Emma would be replaced and Becky was tasked with looking out for the new girls whilst Ceci and Nicole tried to work out where Ben kept his stash, by watching him as subtly as they could.

A two-hour drive in tense silence, three stops at service stations.

"Hell, I don't know! Your guess is as good as mine. I'm thinking inside pocket of his jacket, but that's just because the outside pockets seem too superficial, they look like stuff would fall out of them easily…"

The two new girls stared at them with baffled expressions.

Becky attempted to grin at them and look reassuring, but she knew she was coming across as a bit unhinged.

A university town, the hotel on the outskirts, the smell of it now so familiar it seemed to fragrance their dreams. Yet the new girls were suitably impressed, just like the old girls had been so long ago, it felt that way, anyway, like another, more naïve, lifetime.

"Wow!" They muttered wandering about the lobby. "Fancy!"

Ben removed his jacket and left it draped across his suitcase. The heat in the hotel was shocking after the frigid air outside. Nicole looked at Ceci, and Ceci edged closer and closer.

She was standing right next to Ben's jacket, her heart hammering in her chest, when Ben turned around and lobbed their keys at them.

"You, Becky, are now the new Sammy!" Ben chortled, finding himself hilarious. "For room allocation purposes, I mean!"

It was at that very moment that Becky realised she was not immune, that she could be as much of a victim as the others, and the realisation of that caused a seeping coldness to edge over her body despite the overheated hotel.

"Oh!" She said in the lift, and then little else.

"I know what you're thinking," said Ceci glancing at Becky's ashen face when they entered their room, "But I don't think he'll target you, he doesn't have pics of you, nothing to blackmail you with."

"He's acting nasty because we don't seem like we're scared, which is what he wants, it's a power play."

"I'm scared!" Ceci laughed mirthlessly.

"He can't believe we're back on another tour, he's thrown by it."

"But shouldn't he be glad? I mean that he has another opportunity to get to us?"

"Yes, but I think he suspects something, some rebellion on our part, that's why we've got to be on our guard. Also, he scuppered his own plans by getting sick himself at the end of the last tour. They definitely had something planned…"

"By 'them' you mean, Ben and Peter?"

"That we know of, yes, but there are others too. We have to be aware of that, of any men."

"Excellent, that narrows it right down!"

The girls were sitting on the two bigger beds smoking. The TV was on in case anyone was listening to them speak through the door. There was a print above one of the beds of a river trailing through cornfields.

"I miss Emma." Commented Becky sadly.

"Same, but I'm glad she's away from this, she wasn't coping."

"We need to stay in touch with her, with Sammy too, we need to make sure that no one spirals downwards."

"I can't wait to tell them! When we get him, I mean!"

"What if we don't though? There's a real chance of that, what if they get to us instead first?"

Ceci still had the squashed baggie in the pocket of her jeans. She was still wearing the jeans, albeit with the button and zip undone and the waistband gaping to relieve the pain in her stomach.

"We can't think like that, we can't give up before we even start!"

The Beginning of the End

7.30pm and the girls gathered next to the van in the frigid air of a clear night. Above their hotel, a galaxy of stars glimmered.

"Well, would you look at that?" Ben gestured towards the sky with his cigarette, grinned at the new girls, ignored the old girls, and Becky thought of the teeth of the big bad wolf, the illustrations in a book of fairytales that she still owned, somewhere in her room at home.

She gulped and wished she was back in London with her parents. No money was worth the stress of this.

That evening of work was fine. It was a welcome distraction helping the new girls get into the swing of things. They were shocked by how the old team just lobbed t-shirts at everyone they saw. The pubs were full of students, the atmosphere relaxed.

"But where is Ben?" They asked, more than once. "Doesn't he come to check?"

"Almost never, he just sits in the van, don't worry about it."

Sharon and Helga shrugged at each other. Ceci, seeing this, felt a terrible pity and envy combined. It seemed to her, then, that the two of them still possessed some innocence that the others had lost.

Back at the hotel, Peter was standing in front of the reception desk with his back towards it. His blond hair was flattened against his small skull with a slick of gel.

He smiled, with his dry lips terribly stretched, and put out his hands as if in welcome and the new girls smiled back uncertainly.

"Who is this?" Helga whispered.

"This is my great friend, Peter!" Ben emerged behind them, his booming voice engulfing the room.

Nicole, Ceci, and Becky stood close together and touching; the sides of their arms, their hips. The cold had come inside with them; it was in their bones. It was in the goosebumps on their skin.

Becky felt lightheaded suddenly.

"Let's welcome the new girls with a drink!"

Ben ushered them into the bar area, which always looked the same in these hotels. Orange lighting glimmered against the shiny surfaces and flattered the skin.

"Cocktails?" Peter stood poised to order. He was wearing an expensive suit, ill-fitting nevertheless. Skinny, he was, with a bulging belly, like a snake after the consumption of a meal.

"No thank you!" The 'old' girls said in unison, their voices sounding both desperate and prim.

Helga and Sharon looked surprised and confused.

"Yes please!" they both said.

"Here's a table for us!" Boomed Ben. It was one of those alcoves with a circular sofa seat and he sat at it with his bulky arms stretched out across the top of the seats.

"Come join me!" He cajoled loudly. His grin had evaporated.

"I feel sick!" Whispered Becky and found herself rooted to the spot.

"Nothing can happen now, we'll get a juice," Whispered Nicole softly close to her ear. "We'll watch the bar girl pour it."

The three of them sat to one side of Ben, tense and upright and ready to bolt with their glasses of juice. On the other side sat Helga and Sharon and Peter with their cocktails, replete with umbrellas and cherries.

"Some people," Said Peter pointedly, "are no fun! You guys need to relax, why not? All this money you must have saved by now, doesn't that make you happy?"

"Are you a kind of travelling manager?" Asked Becky, apropos to nothing, her voice emerging hollow.

"I mean you pop up in all these hotels, and I understand you are a manager in one of them, do you manage all of the others too?"

"What Peter does and where he does it," said Ben, "Is none of your concern." His voice had changed to a low ominous growl and the atmosphere had thickened unpleasantly.

The new girls sensed it too. They glanced at each other with their eyes wide. They weren't afraid yet but they were concerned.

"I feel sick!" Said Becky quickly, "Sorry, I'd better go to the room now!"

Ceci and Nicole jumped up with her, grabbed their cigarettes from the table and almost ran out of the bar and towards the stairs.

Once in the room, they barricaded the door with a chair and lay down on the beds panting. Somehow it was difficult to breathe and not just because of all the smoking.

"Sharon and Helga must think we're nuts!"

"Sharon and Helga have far bigger problems than they realise, he could be drugging them as we speak!"

They turned off the harsh overhead light and even the bedside lamps and got into their beds, their eyes wide and terrified, watching shapes form in the gloom.

"We've got to get him before he gets us." Said Nicole into the darkness.

"Tomorrow" Said Ceci, her voice barely audible, "or it might be too late."

"Can't we just go home?" That was Becky, "I mean, sneak out, get a taxi to the train station…"

"Maybe that would save us, Becky," Nicole's voice was low but determined in the darkness, "But it wouldn't avenge the others, all the girls he's targeted thus far and who he, they, I should say, have yet to target. Remember, he has photos of me and Ceci…"

"But the others will still have those photos, even if he's out of the picture!"

"I know, but Ben is the one of the top dogs, one of the chief wolves, I feel that quite strongly, and we have a real chance at getting him. We can't possibly target all the arseholes unfortunately, much as I'd love to."

Somehow, they slept, waking late to another clear wintry azure sky. The window of their room overlooked a strip of grass, a copse of trees and a main road. The grass was covered in a sparkling frost and a tiny fluffy yapping dog was running across it, back and forth, joyfully.

They had already decided not to leave the room until that evening, dread sat in them all, a hard ball in the pit of their stomachs. Ceci, whose stomach was sensitive at the best of times, suffered terrible cramps and spent most of the day lying flat on her back, picturing the little baggie of toxic powder in the pocket of her purple jeans, and hoping desperately that she would get an opportunity to exchange it for the one that was in Ben's jacket pocket.

Early afternoon, Helga phoned from the room next door and asked if she and Sharon could come over.

They both looked pallid and hungover when they came in.

"Big night, was it?" Nicole peered at them warily, as they slumped on one of the bigger beds next to Ceci, who struggled to a sitting position to make room.

"Yeah, we feel really rough, like *really* rough."

"How much did you drink?"

"Only two of the cocktails, I guess they must have been really strong."

Ceci sighed deeply and rolled her eyes. She didn't want to deal with this now. Nicole had no idea what to say so remained silent, she turned deliberately and looked out of the window. There was a different dog on the strip of frosted grass then, an Alsatian, older and sedate, just walking along demurely next to his owner.

Becky was napping, curled onto her side.

"We wanted to ask you girls, what your problem is with Ben, and also that Paul guy? Don't say 'nothing', we know that something is going on!"

"We can't tell you yet." Nicole's head whipped around and she stared at Helga who had spoken, her gaze hard and impenetrable.

"I promise we will, as soon as we can, trust us, OK?"

The girls looked confused, a bit frustrated, but nodded.

"Now let's chill and find a nice, relaxing film to watch."

The Last Night

They met at 7.30 once again under the clear sky and some of them sent their prayers to the stars.

Ben drove them to a couple of pubs and then to a massive club, one of those with multiple levels.

Nicole and Ceci held hands as they went in, they gripped tightly. He followed them, (unusual that was, and sinister) and yelled at them in the foyer.

"What is this hand holding crap? You have to split up, you know that! Nicole off you go, first floor with you, go find the stairs!"

He pushed her forcefully into the throng of bodies already bopping about just past the entrance to the ground floor. She stumbled and fell and by the time she looked back he had gone. The thunderous beat of the dance music drowned out their footsteps, drowned out their voices. The others had already disappeared into the crowd.

"You are coming with me." He said to Ceci, his hand tight on her upper arm. She missed Nicole already with a sadness that was already soaking into her bones. Ceci wished that there was more time, that she had said goodbye. Nobody else heard Ben speak and nobody saw him manhandle Ceci back out of the club again and drag her back to the van. Ceci heard a light buzzing at that moment in her head. She thought of Sammy, the way that she had looked hard when they first saw her, Emma and Becky, their faces, their innocence. She pictured Nicole and Chantal and then her parents and her siblings. She couldn't remember clearly what they looked like and then panic came. Her mind was doing that thing it did before you were about to die, because that is what it believed was about to happen, and she knew that.

In the van, he dragged her and then pushed her onto the passenger seat and went round opened the door and sat next to her. Within seconds, he had screeched out of the parking lot and pulled up into some secluded spot behind thick bushes and industrial-sized bins.

Nicole dashed out of the club into the parking lot, dizzy, panting, but the van had gone.

 Ben put on the overhead light in the front seat and thrust a pile of photographs into Ceci's hand. She knew what they were because of what Sammy had told them, but still it was shocking to see, shocking that it was actually happening, all that they had both feared and predicted, but she was crying so much that she couldn't see clearly, just the pink and brown blurs of naked flesh.

There was a glass bottle of lemonade on the floor at her feet.

Through the windscreen, the stars were beautiful.

"I just have to take a piss, don't go anywhere." He guffawed coldly and opened the door. He headed to the back of the van, there were shrubs there, undergrowth, the bins.

It took Ceci a second for her brain to register that he had gone without his jacket and some more long, painful, seconds for her shaking hands to respond to her brain's command to substitute the baggie inside his jacket with the one inside the pocket of her jeans.

Then he was back, the damp upon him, forcing her to drink the lemonade which tasted chemical as she knew it would, she gagged on it but swallowed it down.

And for minutes nothing happened and Ben started to drive, the rock music blaring as if it was just an ordinary drive, and Ceci felt a bubble of hilarity rise in her. The knowledge came to her that she off her head in a way that she had never been before. Her vision was blurred, the glare of lights came towards them and then receded. He drove with a grimace on his face which could have been a smile, an expression of triumph anyway.

It was just before Ceci passed out, that, with closed eyes, she sensed the van slow and stop. Layby, said a voice in her head. Then he started driving again, and Ceci was absent.

It took a few minutes for the poison he had just snorted to bring him down, and in that time, he was driving erratically, but ever closer to their destination, the room with the men in it, the paying customers.

He never got there and neither did Ceci.

He collapsed at the wheel and the van veered off the road and straight into a tree.

The heavy crunch of hot metal on bone.

They both died immediately, on impact.

EPILOGUE

The girls barely recognised each other when they met.

Well, of course, five years had passed. They had kept in touch sporadically during that time, but with phone calls only. Without acknowledging it, there was a silent understanding between them, for years, that meeting in person would be too painful.

Trauma was there certainly, but also guilt.

A café had sprung up in the park between the two bridges crossing the Thames, the same park that Emma had traversed in desperation to get rid of her portfolio all those years ago. It wasn't a coincidence; she had suggested the spot.

A day in late Spring. As usual, the weather in London was variable, but investment had been bestowed on the area in recent years and the park was ablaze with a wondrous selection of flora.

The café was of the modern variety; over-priced and vegetarian, but cleaner than cafes used to be, with attractive, brightly-coloured, wooden furniture.

The girls sat outside, although it was chilly, and tried not to stare at each other in the unforgiving daylight.

They all looked very different, but in Sammy, the transformation was the most extreme. Her hair was now a glossy brown bob, her face subtly but perfectly made up. Her newly slim body was encased in a smart, but fashionable suit, befitting of a young business owner, which she was.

Sammy now owned and operated three beauty salons, popular with models, actors and the 'in crowd.'

"My friends and I go to the branch closest to us all the time!" Enthused Becky, "Well done you!"

"It wasn't quick or easy, it is only recently that I've really started turning a profit." Said Sammy soberly. "Of course, rents in London being what they are, that takes a huge chunk…"

"Do you live on your own?"

"Oh yes, that was always extremely important to me. I needed to get away from my mother, you all know that."

She looked at their faces and they all nodded.

"I moved out as soon as I feasibly could and now, I have a little studio in Battersea. It's tiny, but it's all mine and it's super secure."

Again, they all nodded, their faces serious. Sammy talked some more about the security features and the alarm system and they listened with uncommon interest.

They were all very interested in security features.

"I saw that musical you were in last year, Becky!" Piped up Nicole after a break in conversation, "It was great, I didn't know that you could dance!"

"Well, I couldn't really, not for ages, and after…well, I had already realised that I needed to add to my skillset to make myself more employable as an actress…"

"I remember you were already taking dancing classes…"

"Yes, and after," She swallowed, "I took more, more intensely, and singing, classes for musical theatre mostly, and it did work. I started getting work in musicals, lowly positions usually but recently, in the last year or two I have been getting better roles…"

"Are you still with your parents?"

"Oh yes. They like me to stay at home, we all get on, it's comfortable there, seems little reason to move out…"

"Fair enough."

Becky of all of them, had changed the least physically, she looked perhaps more glossy, more sophisticated, but fundamentally, she was unchanged.

"What about you Nicole?"

Nicole looked extremely trendy and fashionable, but noticeably older. She had aged beyond her years. There were deep grooves under her eyes, obvious in the starkness of the harsh daylight, and the skin around her mouth was developing the suggestion of smokers' lines. Out of all of them, she was the only one who still smoked.

"Oh, same old, same old, still modelling, still on the estate, still with my mum."

"How is your mum?"

"Frail, more frail, I mean. We have a full-time carer now, she's there all day. My mum never…I mean my mum really struggled after what happened to Ceci, she…"

Nicole stopped; her voice was breaking.

"We all miss her." That was Emma. She leant over and placed her small hand over Nicole's. "I put her into my paintings all the time. Mostly indirectly, but she's always there."

"Yeah, I went to see your last exhibition, it's really impressive!" Said Becky

"Thanks. I can't seem to paint anything except water though, so it's a bit limiting, but still…"

"The sketch that…the river sketch that you did when…I saw that…it became a trio right? Three paintings in a series?"

"It's called a triptych, yes…it came to me when…well after what had happened…I called it 'Ceci'."

"I saw, I…" Nicole started crying silently. She let the tears course down her face and make grooves in her foundation.

"I will never forgive myself, not as long as I live, I let him push me into that club and I knew what he was going to do, I knew but I didn't fight for her…"

"How could you fight?" Exclaimed Becky, "How could we? The size of him alone? All that pent-up violence in him? We were doomed. We were stupid to think we could ever take him on, bring him down, that was our fault, but don't blame yourself, I was there too, remember? I was right there, just in front of you, in that club…"

"But she was my best friend! It was my stupid plan!" Nicole sobbed.

"We were powerless, that was the thing. They presumed that because we were well-paid for that ridiculous job, that we were amenable to anything, that we had to put up with anything. We were helpless because we were young and poor and they knew it and they exploited it."

That was Emma. More than anything, looking at her then, she resembled an earnest student. No make-up, plain glasses, her hair a natural mousey brown. She had told them she shared a flat with a couple of other artists, that she was finally happy.

"You know the whole gang of them got arrested after, right? That was down to us, so we can be proud, we should be proud! When they looked through Ben's car, they found the photographs and well…they went from there…"

"I know, they must have called us all, right?" Becky looked around and the others nodded.

Nicole sighed, but she had stopped crying.

"Three of the drivers involved, that creepy client from the training day, Peter, and that's just the ones we saw and knew of, there were many others apparently. The ones who raped the drugged girls. Seven of the promo girls came forward in the end. Five of them testified."

"They asked me, I couldn't. I just…I could barely function." Said Nicole.

"Me neither…I couldn't do that to my parents."

"There was no way I could have testified. I just needed to forget it all." Said Sammy firmly. "I needed to forget it all completely."

"I was…I was in a bad place…" Emma said. "They wouldn't have been able to reach me anyway."

The others nodded sympathetically. They knew that she was in a psychiatric ward for a while.

"They totally abandoned that promotion, didn't they?"

"Did we ever find out what it was for?"

"Nope, no idea."

THE END

Printed in Great Britain
by Amazon